DISCOVERED DENIAL

DISCOVERED DENIAL

JULIE BAWDEN DAVIS

Roses
A R E
RED
PUBLISHING

ACKNOWLEDGMENTS

As they say, it takes a village. Here's my village. I'm supremely grateful to each of these fabulous people!

ARC Reading Gems
Julie Schlueter
Tara Bradley
Angela Barnes
Heather Wamboldt
Kery Bailey
Trish Darrenkamp
Marilyn Smith
Lisa Starkey
Carolyn Overcash
Susa Fraccaroli

Pros
Sharon Whatley, editing
Judy Bullard, cover design
Kayla Curry, logo design
Kyle Kane, logo design
Sabrina Wildermuth, design consultation
Jeremy Davis, book design

For all who have conquered the seemingly unconquerable and have found themselves once again.

Iris Avena climbed into her yellow Toyota Corolla, slammed the door and let the torrent of tears that had threatened to explode since that afternoon break free. It was quiet here at midnight in the newspaper's back parking lot. Good. No one would see her.

Oh, how excited she'd been to be a journalist when she started five years ago! To save the world with her writing, or at least some corner of the world. But with the newspaper business in the toilet, she'd be lucky if she had a job next week. The publisher had laid off more reporters today. She wasn't one of them. Yet. But a lot of good journalists with much more experience than Iris had been let go. Now she was the senior investigative reporter. Seriously? She should still be studying under veteran journalist Henry Kincaid, who got canned today. Instead, she stayed late to take over where he left off on an article.

Iris rifled around in her purse, seeking a tissue to mop up the tears. She finally found a fast food napkin, then dried her eyes and blew her nose. Flopping her head back on the car's seatback, she gazed out at the loading dock that led to the newsroom's shipping and receiving area. The doors were closed on this mild Southern California September night. She was about to start her car and head home, when a truck lumbered by and headed toward the receiving dock. Tomorrow's edition wouldn't be going out until at least three a.m., so what was a truck doing here at midnight?

Keeping her eyes on the truck as it pulled up to the loading dock, she pressed the button on her glove compartment box, reaching in and locating her binoculars. Peering through them, she watched as two men hopped out and went to the rear of the truck. From her vantage point, she saw one of them pull up the back of the truck as the sound of metal on metal punctuated the quiet night. The other man made a phone call on his cellphone.

If this was a scheduled delivery, someone would be in receiving waiting for them. And even more weird was the fact that there didn't seem to be a company name on the truck. Why the cloak and dagger, she wondered? Iris's heart rate hitched up a notch, and she felt her senses go into high alert.

After a minute or so, the newspaper's receiving door opened and Ignacio Munoz, head of receiving, walked onto the loading dock. He signaled the two men, and one of them jumped into the back of the truck. She wished she could hear them, but she couldn't risk attracting attention by opening her door or turning on her car to lower the window. Her pulse raced as the driver and Ignacio conferred. Then Ignacio pulled a large envelope out of his back pocket and handed it to the other man. She quickly trained the binoculars onto the envelope and gasped at the contents. Money. Lots of it. Anything aboveboard would go through proper channels and include a bill of lading, and no cash would exchange hands.

Iris leaned forward and watched as the men began removing packages from the back of the truck. There were about six or seven of them, and they appeared heavy by the way the men were lugging them. Once they finished unloading, one man pulled the back of the truck shut, and they hopped back in. She watched Ignacio stack several of the packages onto a hand trolley and wheel them into shipping and receiving while the truck backed up and turned around. Before the headlights of the truck struck her car, she crouched down in her seat, her heart thudding in her temples.

She waited until she heard the vehicle rattling down Grand Avenue. When she sat up, the door to receiving was closed.

Iris had never met Ignacio in person but hadn't heard anything negative about him. She'd have to ask some of her sources at the paper tomorrow. Then she realized that one of the main people she would have asked was Henry. Iris sighed and put away the binoculars. She was tired. Most likely there was a perfectly rational explanation for what she'd just seen, although she couldn't think what that could be. Iris turned her car on and made her way out of the parking lot onto the street. She needed to get home and check on Jake, who hopefully hadn't pitched a fit for her mama when it was time for bed tonight, as had been his MO recently.

Joey Landau needed to make a quick decision. Either head to the newspaper loading dock where there might be some evidence left behind after the exchange he'd just witnessed or follow the woman he'd seen peering through binoculars during the drug drop. Something told him he should follow the Corolla. He waited until she turned onto Grand and then drove his way out of the shadows of the trees where he'd been observing from his Jeep. As he tailed the woman's car, he jotted down her license plate number in the notebook on the passenger seat.

Was she going to meet up with one of the truck drivers? Joey wondered. Could she be a girlfriend checking up on her boyfriend? If so, she could definitely prove useful if Joey could get her alone.

Before long, she made her way into a quiet Santa Ana neighborhood composed of 1950s tract homes. Joey stayed back at a distance. When he saw her pull into the driveway of a small house, he cruised by as slow as possible. There was a full moon, so he got a good look at her as she got out of her car and glanced his way. Long brown hair, and she stood up straight. He couldn't wait to tap his buddy at the DMV and find out who the brown-haired beauty was. She had just made this undercover op a whole lot more interesting.

Joey hung up the phone and began doodling in his notebook. So, her name was Iris Avena. An investigative journalist. But why would she investigate her own paper?

He glanced at the clock. Five a.m. He'd only managed about three hours of shut-eye until wondering about the mystery woman had him calling his contact. Joey didn't have to be at the meet for at least three hours. No point in trying to sleep, though. Easier to keep awake on caffeine pills, coffee and the jolts of adrenaline that came with the under-cover narcotics terrain.

Joey stood up, checking himself out in the mirror. Dark circles under his eyes, and his black hair an unruly mop, as his pop used to say.

This time he had insisted with the brass that he have a safe haven to go home to each night. Somewhere all his own to crash. The last op required that he date and live with the cartel boss's daughter. That meant being someone else 24/7, which exhausted him. And it got really messy when the Santa Ana PD arrested her father and brothers. He felt like an asshole every time he thought about how things ended with her.

Joey decided to get himself some java and then gear up and head to the ring. Belting it out with his trainer would help him focus and center for today. It was going to be a long, tough one.

Iris awoke to a grin and a giggle. "What are you doing munchkin? And is that pancakes I smell? I don't recall giving the okay on pancakes on a school day."

"The boy wanted pancakes. Kept talking about them. I made them to quiet him." Her mother, Sara, stood in the doorway of Iris's bedroom, spatula in hand, an apron covering her pajamas. "You got in late last night, *hija.*" It was a statement, but Iris knew it was interlaced with questions.

"They let go of more of the newsroom, Mama. I'm in charge now, and it's going to mean a lot more work."

Her mother's eyebrows raised. "*La jefa, hija? Que bueno.*"

"The boss by default. I don't know if that's so good, Mama, but, yes, I'm the head of the investigative unit now."

"Then you can make the rules, no? How about your first rule is that you sit down and eat a good breakfast with your son and mother?"

Jake stood up on Iris's bed and began jumping his wiry five-year-old body up and down as he shouted, "Eat breakfast with us, Mommy!" Iris reached up and grabbed her son by the arm and pulled him down onto the bed next to her. "As soon as I give you a good kiss or two or ten."

"No!" squealed her son, his brown curls bouncing as she moved in to kiss him on the cheeks. "There, we're done. Let me get dressed, and I'll be right there. You get dressed, too."

Jake raced out of her room, nearly knocking her mama down as he did so.

Her mother eyed Iris. "You're upset, *hija.*"

Iris sat up and leaned against the wall, pushing back her hair. "I've worked for so many years to be a journalist, and now newspapers are doing terrible. They're letting go of the writers with more seniority, because they pay them more, but who knows what will happen next."

"Remember the time you taught yourself to ice skate?"

Iris recalled the experience, which involved falling onto her butt on the hard ice over and over in the rink while her friends hung out at the beach. Finally, she nodded.

"I asked you why you wanted to ice skate in Southern California, *recuerdas?*"

"I remember."

"You said you wanted to prove to yourself you could do it. And when the rink closed, you found another one farther away. You took the bus there every Saturday morning on your own. I'm going to feed the boy. Hurry up before he eats all the syrup."

After her mother left, Iris thought about last night and what she'd seen. How she wished she could pass this by Henry. At least she got to start the day with a bright spot before going to what was left of the newsroom. Breakfast with the two most important people in her life.

Joey threw his gym bag into his jeep and hopped in. It was nearly 7 a.m. Royce was usually booked solid all day long, but if he hurried, he could catch him at the ring to do a little sparring before he started for the day. Whenever Joey found him without a client, Royce would teach him a few more moves. But Royce was much more than a boxing trainer for Joey. He was a lifeline. The older man had helped pull Joey out of the dumpster he had dived into.

Technically, Joey wasn't supposed to be seeing anyone from his real life. That's what deep undercover required. But Joey got wobbly when he didn't see Royce. Started thinking about drinking again. Seeing Royce was a chance he had to take. He'd warned Royce, though. Told him about the risks and gave him an out. The old guy just shrugged and replied, "If it's my turn to meet my maker, I'm ready. Don't you worry about me, Joey. I promised your pop I'd watch over you. I ain't about to stop now."

As he drove toward the gym in downtown Santa Ana, Joey thought about the journalist again. What was she up to right now, he wondered?

Did she have a family? Most likely, since she lived in a house. Trouble was, from his vantage point, she'd seen too much. Or maybe he had it all wrong and she worked for Ignacio to keep tabs on the merchandise coming in. Why else would she be in the newspaper's backlot at midnight when a truck delivered several kilos of black tar heroin with a street value of forty million?

3

Joey found Royce at his gym's decades old boxing ring tightening one of the ropes. Without turning his head, the older man said, "You're in earlier than usual. Good. You can help me."

Dropping his gym bag on the floor, Joey approached. "You going to retie that? Rope's getting old. Maybe it's time for a new one."

"I'm old, too, and I might have lost most of my hair, but you don't see me cashing it in. Now get on the other end and pull while I tie."

"Yes, sir."

Royce grunted as he tied. He wore his usual uniform for the gym. A sleeveless white undershirt and black sweats. Though he had a slight paunch, the older man's arms were still muscular, and he could lay one of the meanest punches Joey had ever felt. Back in the day, Royce had been a welterweight champion. There was a time when Joey thought about trying professional boxing, but joining the police force won out.

When Royce finished tying, both men let go. Smacking the top of the rope, Royce seemed pleased when it sprang back readily. Then he turned to Joey and gave him a good look over.

"What's eating you?"

"Nothing."

"You're not hitting the sauce, are you?"

"I told you, I'm not going down that road again ever. It's just work stuff."

Royce grabbed some gloves from a nearby table and pulled them on. "Work stuff we can hammer out in the ring."

Joey nodded, reaching down and unzipping his bag, pulling out his gloves and yanking them on.

Lifting the rope, Royce climbed into the ring while Joey did the same. When the two men faced one another, Joey responded by tensing and raising his arms, but Royce didn't mirror him. Instead, he asked, "You ever think about quitting?"

Joey lowered his arms. "What? Work?"

"Yeah. All those drugs you're around. That can't be easy."

Joey's shoulders slumped. "We here to talk about my sobriety or do some sparring?"

"You've come a long way, is all I'm saying. I'd hate to see you backslide. That last time. In the hospital."

Joey made as if to give him a couple quick jabs. "How about we make a deal? If it gets too rough, I'll transfer to another department at the PD. That make you happy?"

Royce pretended to block him. "What'll make me happy is to lay your ass down in the ring, but I'll take that."

Joey took his stance, holding the gloves in front of his face. "Maybe you can get a two for two."

Royce grinned and swung the first punch.

Iris drove into the *Orange County Recorder* parking lot wondering how long it would be before she crashed from her pancake breakfast sugar high. Her mother loved to spoil Jake, and Iris let her. She knew it gave her purpose since her father died a few years before. Having the help also made being a single mother a lot easier for Iris.

As she parked, Iris glanced at receiving in the morning sunlight. A newsprint truck was parked next to the loading dock now. She shook off last night's memory and headed into the newsroom, bracing herself for another day of uncertainty.

After showering and changing into jeans and a jet blue tank top, Joey checked his reflection in the dingy mirror of the gym's small bathroom. He grimaced when he eyed the gang tattoo on his bicep. That would be a bitch to have removed once this case was over. He thought about Royce's concerns. It had been getting dicey lately, especially with all the drugs and alcohol constantly being thrust at him.

On his way out, he waved to Royce, who was with a client. Flinging his gym bag in his jeep, Joey hopped in and revved the engine, pulling out of the parking lot and heading to a warehouse in downtown Costa Mesa.

For six months now, he'd been deep into this case. It wasn't until recently that the leader, Raul Ortega, a sly prick with a twisted sense of humor, trusted him enough to let him walk into headquarters without first getting a once-over by one of his henchmen. Except for Raul, most of the gang was better at muscle than thinking things through. Joey had proven himself an expert strategizer for the gang. And another member of the PD, who had been undercover in the gang for two years now, had vouched for Joey.

"Hey homey, you're late," said Raul, when he walked into the warehouse. The crew used the space as a garage and gathering spot. There was a table, where they sat on important occasions, a set of couches, a flat screen, and a makeshift kitchen. Joey started to reply when the warehouse door opened on the far end of the room and Marco came roaring in on his Harley, the engine's rumbling shaking the walls.

Raul shook his head. "Shit. I told him that's an old man's bike, but he don't listen. You ever seen a Hells Angel, homey? They're about eighty-years-old." Raul laughed at his own joke, exposing his front teeth, one of which was capped in gold. He wore a blue bandana on his shaved head, and a gold chain with a cross hung from his neck.

Joey felt his back stiffen at the comment. His pop had been a Harley rider, but he kept a smooth smile on his face. "I like a roof over my head when I'm driving, but that's just me."

"So, what you see last night?" Raul asked, motioning for Joey to sit down on the couch across from him.

Marco walked up then, easing his large frame into a faded recliner.

Joey reached into his pants pocket and pulled out a packet of cigarettes and a lighter. "The Townsend gang," he said. He lit the cigarette. "I recognized one of the men. Must have dropped off at least eight kilos."

"*Hijole*. We need to shut them down," complained Marco. "They're cutting into my sales."

Raul shot Marco a dark look. "My sales."

Marco's face reddened.

"Get the crew together," Raul ordered Marco. "We'll intercept the delivery tonight. We want the mules alive, so I can find out who's behind this bullshit. Anyone gets in the way, get rid of them."

Joey's mind flashed to the journalist.

4

Iris sat at her desk in the nearly empty newsroom staring at her computer screen. She was supposed to be coming up with ideas for some investigative pieces, but she kept picturing the scene in the parking lot last night. She couldn't just pretend she hadn't witnessed anything. But who to tell? She had no idea how far this ran. She could call her Aunt Joanna, who worked for the FBI. Trouble was, her aunt was protective, and she'd probably insist Iris stay away from this. Iris decided to visit shipping and receiving and do some poking around herself. Glancing at the clock on her computer, she noted she had two hours before the staff meeting. Plenty of time.

Iris walked the quiet halls toward receiving, missing the days when the *Recorder* had been bustling. She remembered the electric feeling she had walking into the building for the first time, a new hire at twenty-five. She used to feel her blood racing through her body at the prospect of working on articles that would be published in a real newspaper. She could never have imagined, five years later, how the industry would take a turn.

When she arrived at shipping and receiving, Iris found no one around. She checked the room for any sign of the packages she'd seen last night. As she leaned down to look under the shipping table, a voice behind her made her jump. "Can I help you with something?"

Iris peered up to find Ignacio standing there, hands on hips.

She grabbed the edge of the lightweight sweater she'd thrown on that morning and said, "I heard a button pop off my sweater and possibly go under the table there." She pointed. "But I don't see it."

Ignacio's face relaxed slightly. "I'll let you know if I find it."

Iris smiled. "Thanks. I'm expecting a shipment of designer sunglasses. They're counterfeits. I'm writing a story about them. I work in the investigative section."

"I'll keep an eye out." Ignacio gave her a big smile that said, you can go now.

"Great. I'm on the third floor."

"I know."

On her way back to the newsroom, Iris decided to check out the parking lot again that night. This time she'd bring a camera.

Joey didn't like this. The gang was planning an all-out war with the Townsend gang in a few minutes at the newspaper. There would be security guards to deal with, for one. And it was a pretty populated area. He also hadn't been able to get ahold of his handler at the PD to tell her what was going down. As of now, he was going in alone. If Raul knew how much firepower the other gang had, he wasn't sharing. The Townsend boys were known for leaving no prisoners, so they generally came in guns blazing. Raul refused to talk logistics with Joey. Instead, their leader babbled about how his girlfriend's tamales weren't as good as his mother's. That's the way Raul worked. He liked to keep everyone off their game as much as possible. From what Joey could see, he did it to keep them in line and on their toes.

When it was time to head out, Raul announced, "Remember, homeys, I want the delivery drivers back here alive. The plan is we hold onto the product for now. We need to be certain where it comes from and have

Eduardo test it out. We'll beat it out of them who they been selling to." Raul shoved his gun in the back of his pants and clapped his hands, demanding they hurry. "*Ándale!*"

When they arrived at the *Recorder's* ten-story building twenty minutes later, Raul instructed, "Park out front. We go in on foot."

Marco shut off the van's engine under a dim streetlamp, and they all headed for the back parking lot. Joey's heart lurched when he saw the yellow Toyota.

"You seen that car here last night?" Raul asked him.

"First I seen of it," Joey lied. "It's got to be someone working late. Or they're leaving the car here for the night."

"Marco, check it out," ordered Raul.

"I'll do it," Joey said. He wondered if he'd offered too quickly, because Marco and Raul both gave him a quizzical look. Then Raul grinned and said, "You want some exercise, go ahead. Just make it quick. If there is anyone in the car, finish them off. We don't want no witnesses."

Joey stayed low as he headed to the car, hoping that the woman wasn't in it, but when he was a few yards away, he saw her. He slowed and approached quietly. When he was right next to her window, he tapped lightly, then put his finger to his lips as she gaped up at him. He motioned for her to roll down her window farther, but she shook her head. He tried the car door. Locked.

"What do you want?" she said through the window crack.

"Listen carefully," Joey said in a low voice. "Lie down in the car, and don't let anyone know you're in here. Something very bad is about to go down, and you don't want to get caught in the crossfire." Just then, he heard a truck rumbling toward the parking lot. Joey ran away from the Corolla toward the stand of trees where Raul and the gang lay in wait. As he raced across the lot, he prayed she listened to his advice.

5

Iris crouched down in the seat just as a truck drove by. Since when did bad guys warn people? Maybe he just didn't want her to take photos? She was about to take a peek at what was going on when she heard gunshots that jolted her so much, she bumped her head against the steering wheel.

Ay, Dios mío! What had she gotten herself into?

This was already a shit show, Joey thought. Marco had tried to shoot the driver to stop him from getting back in the cab but instead hit the receiving dock. That gave the driver just enough lead to shoot Marco in the stomach as Raul hit the driver in the arm. The driver still managed to get back in the cab and took off, barreling through the gang as they scattered. No one was making any moves to help Marco. Joey ran to him.

Marco lay on his back moaning, blood soaking the front of his shirt. Joey took off his own shirt and pressed it into Marco's stomach. Then he spied the loading dock, which Ignacio had abandoned once the shooting began. There on the edge lay a package.

"Is he going to be okay?" asked Juan, a wide-eyed young kid who had just been initiated into the gang.

"Press this into his wound. Hard. We gotta keep it from bleeding," Joey instructed him. "The cops will be here any minute. I'll be right back." Just as Joey finished his sentence, sirens blared in the distance. Juan took over while Joey ran to the loading dock and grabbed the package, hoisting it over his shoulder. Relief washed over him when he saw Raul's van heading toward them. As the sirens got closer, the men hoisted Marco into the van. Raul screeched out of the parking lot, soon racing down Grand Avenue away from the approaching flashing lights.

"*Que estupido!*" Raul fumed at Marco, who lay groaning. "How many times I tell you to go to your old man's in the desert and practice shooting, instead of sitting on your fat ass?"

"He needs help," Juan cried.

"He'll be okay. All that fat is good insulation." Raul laughed. "I'm taking him to our doctor." The van careened around a corner. Joey knew he was headed toward Minnie Street, one of the most dangerous barrios in Santa Ana. By the time they pulled in front of a gritty apartment, Marco lay barely conscious. After shutting off the van, Raul glanced back at Marco. "Shit, he better not die on me. He's my best earner."

Joey slid the van door open, and he and Juan carried Marco to the building.

Raul rapped on the door several times, calling out, "*Necesitamos ayuda!*"

A middle-aged Hispanic man opened the door, then stepped back and gestured for them to carry Marco inside. They hoisted Marco onto a metal exam table in a back room lined with glass cases filled with medical supplies. The doctor peeled Marco's blood-soaked shirt off so he could inspect the damage.

At that point, Joey remembered the heroin he'd left in the van. He turned to Raul. "Did you lock the car?"

"No, why?"

"There was a package on the loading dock. I grabbed it—" Before he could finish, Raul was out the door.

Joey found Raul in the driver's seat of the van, a huge grin on his face.

He turned to Joey and said, "I thought tonight was a bust, but it wasn't. *Eres un chingón.*" That was good news for Joey, because it meant, you're a bad ass, in English.

It was an hour before the doctor finished with Marco. He had managed to remove the bullet, stop the bleeding and sew him up. He insisted Marco stay the night for monitoring.

"Juan, stay with him," Raul ordered.

"*Sí, jefe.*" Juan nodded vigorously.

Raul leaned over Marco and said, "Close call, homey, heal up quick. We got work to do." Then he marched out of the building while Joey trailed after him. Once in the car, Raul asked, "How many times you been shot?"

"Once and that was too many," said Joey.

"You said you can shoot, but you didn't shoot tonight."

"Marco beat me to it."

Raul sniggered. "Marco would be lucky to beat an old lady across the street. Why didn't you shoot?"

"I thought you wanted the guys alive. If Marco hadn't shot, I would have cornered the guy and forced him into your car."

Raul shrugged and kept his eyes on the road, staying silent for the rest of the drive back. When they parked the van inside the warehouse, he remarked, "Keep this off the road for a while."

Gloria, Raul's girl, lay stretched out on the couch watching a Spanish novella. She wore a halter top and miniskirt that matched her jet-black hair. When Joey and Raul walked up, she glanced at Joey for a split second, then sprang off the couch and ran to Raul, wrapping herself around him.

"I'm going to bail," said Joey. "See you *mañana.*"

Making out with Gloria already, Raul didn't bother to answer. Joey headed toward his jeep on the street.

After being questioned by the police in the newspaper parking lot for an hour, Iris walked into her living room, set her computer case on the couch, and slid off her shoes. Sara looked up from her magazine and gasped, "*Qué pasó, hija?*"

Iris was about to tell her mother everything, when someone rapped on the front door. Swinging around, her legs began to shake. When she motioned to grab the door handle, her mother cried out, "Check who it is first!"

Her mind numb from the night's drama, Iris couldn't imagine who it could be. She put both hands on the door to steady herself, and peeked through the peephole. What she saw made her gasp. *How did he know where she lived?*

Knocking again, this time more insistently, he called out, "I know you're in there. It's important I speak with you."

6

"Do you want me to call the police?" whispered her mother, who had come up behind Iris.

"No, Mama, it's okay. This is about my work. Go check on Jake."

Sara reluctantly headed toward the bedrooms as Iris took a deep breath and opened the door partway.

"Who are you, and what do you want?"

"My name is Joey Landau. I don't mean you any harm." He held both of his arms up as he said this.

She opened the door a little wider. "If this is about me not pursuing you and your gang..." Iris had no idea where to go from there after blurting that out.

"I'm not—" he started but stopped. "I just wanted to make sure you're okay."

Iris stood up straighter. "I'm fine. You can go now."

Joey looked down at her feet, and she suddenly realized she was standing barefoot. As he gazed at her blue painted toenails, Iris felt a warm rush.

"Is that all?" she asked.

Joey sighed and ran his hands through his glossy black hair. "I'm just making sure you held up during the police questioning."

This guy was beginning to irritate Iris. "Why wouldn't I hold up to the police questioning?" As the words came out of her mouth, she realized his ulterior motive. "So that's why you came? To see what I told the cops."

Joey's eyes followed a moth up to the porch light. "I meant it when I said I wanted to make sure you were okay. Why else would I have warned you at the car tonight?"

He had a good point. "I didn't tell them I saw you, if that's what you're worried about."

Joey's hair fell in his eyes, and he shook it out of them. "Thank you, but can I ask why not?"

"Maybe it's your lucky night. But thanks to you, I've had enough drama to last a year." She motioned to close the door.

"I'd think you'd get a lot of drama in your line of work," he said, which caused her to stop cold.

"And what is my line of work?"

"Investigative journalism. I'll let you go back inside now. It's late." Joey backed up. "Have a good night."

Iris slammed the door harder than she had intended. When she swung around filled with a mixture of irritation and fear, Jake and her mother stood there.

"I thought he was going to the bathroom," Sara started explaining, "but he came out here because he heard your voice."

Iris kneeled and reached out for Jake, pulling him to her for a tight hug. "Go back to bed, munchkin. You have school tomorrow. C'mon, I'll tuck you in."

"Can you sit with me while I go to sleep?" Jake asked, trailing his favorite blanket behind him on the carpeting.

"Of course."

As she sat watching her son drop off to sleep in his bedroom, she thought about the night's events. As far as she could tell, the police weren't clear on what had happened in the parking lot. She told them that she had fallen asleep in her car and woke up when the shooting started. They seemed to believe her story. The truth was, she didn't see anything, because she wasn't looking. She felt foolish admitting that. An investigative journalist should be investigating, not cowering on the floor of her car. Iris sighed. Could she do this? Be an investigative journalist and support her little family? Sara took in jobs sewing *quinceañera* and wedding dresses, and she received social security, but the brunt of paying for the family went to Iris.

Once Jake was asleep, she tiptoed out of his room and almost ran into her mother in the hallway.

"You going to tell me about that man now, *hija?*"

Iris sighed. There was no point in trying to fool her mother. She could read a lie before it was fully formed. When Iris was pregnant with Jake, Sara knew even before Iris was sure. And she also knew who had gotten her pregnant. Her mother wasn't pleased, for good reason. Mark turned out to be a prescription drug addict who couldn't keep a job and disappeared the night before Jake turned one. But her mother never said I told you so. Instead, she surveyed the damage and came up with a plan. Iris could move in with Sara into her childhood home, and Sara would quit her job and take care of Jake.

"Let's talk in the living room," said Iris. When they got to the well-worn couch, Iris wasn't surprised to see two teacups on the coffee table.

"*Té de manzanilla* to calm your nerves," said her mother.

"I can use some nerve calming. *Gracias.*" Iris picked up the warm chamomile tea and took a sip. "And you added honey."

Her mother sipped her own tea, waiting for Iris to begin.

"I'm pretty sure there's something illegal going on at the newspaper. I saw some things I shouldn't have tonight, and then the police came."

Sara sat up. "*La policía?*"

"I told them I didn't see anything."

"Why?"

Iris curled her feet under her legs. "Because I don't really know what's going on. The newspaper has had so much trouble over the last couple of years. I don't want to add to it with misinformation."

Her mother took another sip of tea and set the cup down. "And what does that man have to do with all of this?"

Iris looked beyond her mother at the dining room table, which held her sewing machine and a bolt of white fabric. "He helped me tonight, but he's most likely bad news."

"*Mal noticias* is something you don't need. You have a son to think about."

"I know, Mama. I think about Jake all the time. Believe me."

Joey drove to his apartment, thinking about Iris. There was something about her that made him want to know more. It wasn't just her good looks. He admired her steely nerves. And he couldn't help but wonder if he'd run into her again.

7

Iris sat at her desk in the newsroom the next day looking up information on local gangs. It was eye-opening. In Santa Ana alone, there were three active gangs, each associated with a color. She'd seen Joey and his gang wearing blue tank tops and bandanas the other night at the newspaper. But he just didn't seem like a gang member, she thought. There was something different about him that she couldn't put her finger on. Not to mention that he was cute. But she'd gotten herself mixed up with a not so great guy before. She had learned her lesson.

"Avena, my office, please!" called out her boss, Leonard Smith. Iris exited the website she'd been reading and turned off her monitor.

When she walked into Leonard's office, her breath caught in her throat to see Ignacio from receiving sitting across from her boss.

Iris sat down on the edge of a free chair and waited. Leonard was a tall, thin African American man with spectacles that often perched on the tip of his nose when he consulted his notes. He wore starched white shirts and colorful ties that he'd flip over his shoulder when he examined a newspaper closely. Iris assumed so as not to get newsprint on them.

"I think you know Mr. Munoz from receiving?"

Iris shifted in her seat and glanced at Ignacio, then turned back to Leonard. "Yes."

"We're going to try something a little different, given how many layoffs there have been and the number of empty spots we need to fill."

Iris had no idea where this was going.

"Mr. Munoz, Ignacio, has expressed interest in learning the ropes in terms of photography. In Mexico, where he emigrated from five years ago, he took photos for a newspaper in his hometown of San Felipe."

Iris turned to Ignacio, trying to hide the shock and disbelief she currently felt. "I had no idea."

"Not many people do," Ignacio replied. Was that a smirk pulling on the edges of his mouth, or was she just being paranoid?

"What would you like me to do?" Iris asked.

"Show him the ropes, in terms of the investigative work. He has his job to do in receiving, but it'd be good if he could go out with you on a story today. Maybe that slumlord article we talked about. I'd feel better if you had backup for that one, anyway."

"That's a great idea," she said with more enthusiasm than she felt. "I'm headed for that apartment building on Rosa Linda to interview the tenants. Ignacio could get some photos of the inside of their apartments."

"The photography department can lend you a digital camera for today, Ignacio."

"Sounds good," said Iris, plastering a smile on her face. "I'll give you a report at the end of the day."

While Ignacio went to get a camera, she sat down at her desk and made the motions of preparing to leave, but her mind whirred at the significance of this. Since when did the head of receiving take an interest in investigative reporting? One thing was for sure. It would soon become apparent if Ignacio knew his way around a camera.

Joey pulled a bag of pistachios out of his glove box and ripped them open. He was in the front parking lot of the newspaper monitoring if

Munoz got any suspicious visits during the day. Anything to give him a lead as to what the hell was going on here. He had finally talked to his handler at the PD early that morning and gave her the latest, which wasn't much. He couldn't tell yet if this was a low-level operation that ended at shipping and receiving, or if it ran deeper.

Breaking open a pistachio shell, he popped the nut meat into his mouth. The pistachios kept his hands and mouth busy. He was trying not to smoke so many cigarettes. They had been a lifeline when he quit drinking, but they'd become a crutch. And the truth was, he didn't really like cigarettes. Pistachios, though, he could eat them all day and night. Just then, a yellow Corolla pulled out of the back parking lot. Munoz was in the passenger seat.

Iris wasn't thrilled about being alone in a car with Ignacio. He gave her the creeps, and he was so full of himself. That was what had attracted her to her ex-husband, Mark. Unlike so many men she'd known in her life, he wasn't macho at all. But then he had his own set of problems.

"Don't take any photos unless they agree," said Iris as she pulled up in front of the building. "And we need to get a photo release."

Ignacio nodded.

"Just follow my lead." Iris got out of the car with her notepad in hand and headed up the front stairs. "I have a source who gave me some apartment numbers where the occupants might be open to talking."

Inside, they stepped into a rickety elevator that smelled of urine. She prayed they'd get to the sixth floor safely.

At the door of 636, Iris stopped and listened for a moment, then rapped several times. A young boy answered and peered up at them.

"*Los padres?*" Iris asked if his parents were there, when a woman's voice sounded from within the room. "*Quién es?*"

"We're from the *Recorder, señora*. I know Enrique Cortez. He said you might be open to talking about what it's like to live here?"

A woman came to the door and shooed the boy away. She wore a long, beige dress splattered with grease stains and held a toddler on one hip.

"What do you want?"

Iris introduced them both and explained she was writing an article about the building, in hopes it would bring attention to its disrepair, so the landlord would respond by making improvements. As she spoke, the woman kept stealing glances at Ignacio.

When Iris finished talking, the woman addressed Ignacio. "Haven't I seen you before?"

Ignacio shrugged his shoulders. "I don't think so."

"And what is your name, if I may ask?" Iris inquired.

"Solaria Herrera," she said, switching the toddler to the other hip.

"May we come in and talk to you for the article? Maybe get a few photos of the apartment?"

Solaria hesitated. "I don't want to get in trouble with the landlord."

"We can protect your identity, if you don't want to use your real name."

Solaria glanced at Ignacio again. "*Está bien.*" She stood to the side to let them in.

The living room was strewn with children's toys and clothing. In the nearby kitchen, a mountain of dishes sat in the sink, and the faucet dripped. Iris smelled mildew and fought back a sneeze.

"*Discúlpame,*" Solaria apologized when she realized there was nowhere for them to sit. She rushed to clear off a ratty couch, piling the contents onto a nearby chair. Not wanting to be rude, Iris sat down on the couch while Ignacio began taking photos.

"Solaria, you live here with your children? Anyone else?" Iris asked as the woman sat down on the other end of the couch and set her toddler on the floor beside her, giving him a toy truck.

"Just me and my children, and my younger brother, Juan."

"How long have you been here?"

"I think five years now."

Iris nodded and took notes. At one point during the interview, she glanced over at the chair piled high with the items from the couch, and her heart skipped a beat. There amongst the items was a blue bandana.

8

When they returned to the newspaper a few hours later, Iris felt like taking a bath. The apartments had been filthy and in such disrepair. She hoped her article could bring attention to the landlord's responsibility to provide a humane living environment.

Ignacio had surprised her with his ability with the camera. He took many good photos that they'd be able to use. Maybe he wasn't lying about having been a photographer. Then she recalled Solaria's mention of a brother and the blue bandana. Had Ignacio also seen it?

Joey waited in front of the rundown apartment building as long as possible, but Iris and Munoz didn't come out. Raul had been texting him asking where the hell he was, so Joey finally returned to the warehouse.

When he arrived, Raul was completely pissed off. He was pacing with one of his switchblades in hand. Never a good sign.

"Where you been, homey?"

"Tracking Munoz, so we can figure out where the drugs are coming from."

That calmed Raul down slightly. "Yeah, and what did you find out?"

Joey had a feeling he was being tested, so he decided to tell the truth.

"I followed him to an apartment building on Rosa Linda. He was in there for a while."

Raul nodded and motioned to Juan, who sat on one of the couches. "Juan lives in that apartment house with his sister, Solaria. She just called him. Munoz went to his apartment with some reporter from the *Recorder* and started poking around and taking pictures." Raul held his switchblade up and examined it, then took the edge of his t-shirt and wiped the blade and flicked it shut. "I want you to check out this reporter. Iris Avena. Find out what she knows."

Joey nodded.

"If she's involved with Munoz, we need to remove her from the picture."

Leonard wanted copy as soon as possible, so Iris sat down and started writing. Before long, she became immersed in the plight of those living in the rundown building. One young mother struggled with a little boy who had asthma and was allergic to the mold that seemed to permeate the building. Residents also reported cockroaches running rampant through their apartments.

When she finished with the tenants' side of the story, it was time to try and call the owner of the apartment building again. She'd made numerous calls and left messages, but he was avoiding her. Just as she picked up the phone, someone walked up behind her. Swinging around in her chair, she looked up into Joey's face.

He gestured to the chair next to her desk. "Can I sit down?"

When Iris failed to answer, he said, "I'm not stalking you. I swear. I'm just here to…" Joey trailed off.

Iris waited, fighting the warm feeling that rushed through her whenever she took a good look at him. She noted he hadn't shaved in a couple of days, and even that looked good on him. This time he wore a short-sleeved green shirt and jeans.

"Go ahead and sit down."

"Working on anything interesting?" Joey asked as he took a seat.

"If this is another fishing expedition, forget it."

"It's not. Just making small talk."

Iris leaned back in her chair and folded her arms across her chest. "Okay, answer me this. Where are you from?"

Joey smiled. "You mean what city in Southern California?"

"Sure, start with that."

"I grew up in the San Fernando Valley, but I moved to Orange County when I went to high school, which was fifteen years ago now."

Iris watched him closely as he answered. He appeared to be telling the truth. "You grew up with your parents?" Iris suddenly felt intrusive with the question. "Sorry, it's the reporter in me."

"It's okay," said Joey, whose tense expression had changed to an easier one. "My pop raised me. My mother was an artist from Italy. She left us and went back to Italy when I was a child."

Iris was about to ask another question, when Joey checked a clock on the wall, then leaned close to Iris, his nearness sending a pleasurable tingle up and down her neck. He spoke in a low voice. "I just came here to warn you. I don't know what's going on with you and Munoz, but he's bad news. And there's some dangerous people who don't want you nosing around."

Then Joey stood up and said, "Take care of yourself."

Iris watched as he left the newsroom. Then she wondered what his words meant as a ripple of anxiety raced through her belly.

Joey got in his car and reached for the bag of pistachios, finding it empty. "Damnit," he cussed. What the hell had gotten into him? He'd never told anyone about his mother abandoning him. And here he was blurting it out to a reporter, of all things. He thought about smoking a cigarette, then decided to head to Royce's. Maybe he'd have some free time to let Joey work out some of these kinks before he went back to deal with more of Raul's bullshit.

When he walked into the gym a few minutes later, Joey was glad to see that things were quiet. He found Royce putting away some barbells. His mentor grunted at him. "Little late in the day for a visit."

"I had some free time before going back to work for the night."

Royce turned to face Joey. "Things going okay at work?"

"If you're referring to if I'm okay regarding the booze and drugs. Yes, they're going fine."

"Then what's eating you?"

"Nothing. Like I said, I figured I could iron out some kinks before the night shift."

Royce looked deep into Joey's eyes and squinted. "These ain't kinks from your job. This is about a broad. Who is she?"

Joey was always floored at how intuitive Royce was. "Just a woman involved in my latest case. And it'd be better if she wasn't involved. It's dangerous for her."

"Since when you play the knight in shining armor?"

Joey flung down his gym bag and threw up his arms. "Since never. I don't know. I just hate to see her hurt, is all."

Royce picked up Joey's gym bag and shoved it at him. "I ain't saying that being a knight is a bad thing. Way I see it, it's about time. Put on your gym clothes. We'll get your head on straight."

9

Iris thought about Joey's warning as she parked her car a block from the newspaper that night and took off on foot. She would just stick to the shadows and with any luck figure out what was going on. She had brought her cellphone. If things went sideways, she could call 911. The Santa Ana police station was just a few blocks away.

When she neared the newspaper, a car sped by and pulled into the lot ahead. She tucked her hair into the hood of her black sweatshirt. At the entrance to the parking lot, she checked carefully for signs of anyone, then ran past the empty guard shack into a stand of trees. Moving as close to the loading dock as she dared, she crouched down to wait. She checked the time—11:30. As she did so, she failed to notice someone creeping up behind her until it was too late. A strong arm gripped her throat and squeezed.

"What the fuck are you doing?" Iris heard someone say as she began to feel faint. She sensed struggling behind her, then the arm let go, and she fell to her knees, gasping for air.

"Kill her now, and you'll lead the cops straight here." It was Joey's voice.

Iris scrambled up and tried to bolt, but the man caught her by the sweatshirt and yanked her back. "She's a liability."

Iris looked at Joey's face, but he avoided her eyes. "Let me take her away," he said. "Then there won't be a trace. You got the guys for backup if there's any action."

At Joey's words, terror raced through her veins and she started to scream, but he clamped his hand over her mouth and gave her a look that seemed almost pleading.

The man sniggered. "She your type, homey? Fine. Get rid of her." He pushed Iris into Joey's arms. Joey grabbed her in a vice grip and jerked her forward. "Start walking," he ordered. "And if you scream again, I'll rip your hair out."

When they got to the sidewalk, Joey pulled Iris close and said, "Keep walking. My car is the jeep up ahead. I promise you'll be alright."

Iris nodded. After they got in the jeep, Joey roared down the road, constantly checking his rearview mirror. It wasn't until they reached a quiet street in the city of Tustin that Joey appeared to calm down.

He parked in a carport and pointed to an apartment building. As they made their way silently across the grass and up to a door, Iris had no idea if she could trust him. But she didn't have much of a choice.

Inside, she sat down on a black leather couch, putting her head in her hands as she heard Joey close the front door and begin moving around. He returned and kneeled next to her with a glass. Her nostrils registered orange juice. She looked from Joey to the glass.

"The sugar in the juice will help you get your bearings. It's not going to kill you." He appeared to wince at his choice of words.

When Iris still wouldn't drink, Joey took a big gulp himself. Then he put the glass in her hands. "See, it's fine," he urged, his voice soothing.

Iris exhaled and took a drink of the orange juice, then wiped her mouth with the side of her hand and cleared her throat. It felt raw. "I thought you were going to kill me."

Joey sat back on his haunches and studied her, finally speaking. "You know, you are one obstinate woman. I told you to stay away."

"I don't recall you being my boss," Iris said defiantly, realizing that she sounded like a child.

"You telling me your boss put you up to this?"

Iris took another drink of the orange juice, finishing it off. "He has no idea."

"You always go out on your own? Don't you have a partner or something?"

"I did, but he was fired the other day. Then today my boss paired me with Ignacio. He said Ignacio was a photographer back in Mexico."

"Do you buy that?"

"I don't know what to think anymore. And you never answered my question. Are you planning to hurt me like you said?"

Joey eased into an armchair across from Iris. "I'm not a killer. At least not of innocent people."

"Some gang member you are." Iris snorted, then felt like kicking herself. Was she trying to piss him off so much that he did kill her? Instead of getting mad, Joey burst out laughing.

Iris said indignantly, "I'm glad my impending death is amusing you."

"You're not gonna die. Not on my watch." Joey stood up. "I'm hungry. Want some leftover pizza?"

Iris realized that it'd been hours since she'd eaten. "What kind?"

Joey chuckled again. "A picky hostage. It's pepperoni, onion, and garlic."

Iris watched him dig around in his refrigerator, then pull out a pizza carton. He brought two paper plates over, along with two bottled waters. Placing everything on a coffee table littered with books and several newspapers, he flipped the pizza box open and tore two slices off. The smell was too tempting to resist, so Iris reached for a slice.

"Roma D' Italia," said Joey when Iris nodded in approval. "My favorite Italian restaurant."

"Isn't your boss going to ask for proof that I'm dead?" she asked, mouth full.

Joey looked up. "That idiot, Raul? He's not my boss."

"Then who is?"

"I can't discuss it."

10

If Iris knew Joey was a narcotics officer that would put her in worse danger. Then again, she was in deep right now. Fact was, Joey had no idea what to do next. If he let her go and Raul found out, which would undoubtedly happen, he'd send someone else to kill her. He had to find a way out for her. This was going to be one long night.

"You want my bed or the couch?" he asked, pointing to his bed several yards away in the small studio apartment.

"What? I need to go home. I can't stay here."

"You can't go home. Your life is in danger. I need to figure out what to do next." Just then Joey's cellphone rang. He checked the caller ID and put his finger to his lips, then answered. "Yeah."

"She gone?" Raul asked.

"Yeah."

"Without a trace?"

"Don't worry about it."

"What'd you do with her?"

"It's done, okay. I'll see you tomorrow." Joey hung up the phone and looked at Iris's ashen face.

"I've got a son and my mother," she said. "Are they going to be okay?"

"A son?" That surprised Joey.

"They live with me."

"They'll be fine, as long as you don't contact them."

Iris stood up, knocking the paper plate on her lap to the floor. "My mother will be terrified if she doesn't hear from me! And she'll probably call the police."

"Okay, okay." Joey thought for a moment. "Text your mom and tell her you're going out of town on a story, and you're fine."

Joey watched as she sat back down on the couch and texted.

"How old is your son?"

"He'll be six in two weeks."

"Where's his father?"

"He left when Jake was one."

"Oh, sorry," said Joey, although he found himself secretly glad. Her cellphone buzzed. Iris looked toward him; her brown eyes full of worry. "My mother wants to know where I'm going."

"Tell her that your boss asked that you don't divulge it to anyone, in case of leaks. Not even family."

Iris nodded and texted her mother, then plunked her phone on the coffee table. "What a mess. Please don't tell me I told you so."

Joey smiled. "Where did you want to sleep?"

"On the couch is fine."

"I'll get you a pillow and blanket."

When he returned to the couch, Iris was already lying down. "Thank you for not killing me," she said as she took the blanket and covered herself, pulling it up to her ears.

"I'll be right there if you need me." He gestured to his bed.

Iris watched as Joey double checked the deadbolt on the door and turned off all lights but one small lamp. She listened as he washed up in the bathroom, all the while wondering why he hadn't killed her as ordered. Though she really wanted to insist on going home, she couldn't put her mother and Jake in danger. When he exited the bathroom, Iris tensed, half expecting him to come to the couch, but he got into bed.

Joey listened as Iris shifted on the couch trying to get comfortable. He'd been undercover long enough to know when someone was anxious. She had good reason to be worried about her mother and son. No doubt she was also freaked out about being in the home of a stranger who she thought was a gang member tasked with killing her. After a while, he could tell by her slow breathing that she had fallen asleep. Joey lay in his own bed staring at the ceiling a long time trying to figure out how to get them both out of this mess.

When Joey awoke at the first light coming in from under the shade in his bedroom, he had formed a plan. About to bound out of bed, he remembered Iris was there. That made him smile. Even though she had caused him a lot of trouble, it was nice not to be alone for a change. But wishful thinking wasn't going to get him anywhere, he reminded himself. That's what his last AA sponsor would always say. Iris stirred, then bolted upright and glanced around wild-eyed, until she remembered where she was.

"My sentiments exactly," said Joey quietly. "Coffee?"

"I probably don't need any caffeine, considering that my heart is beating faster than a locomotive, but I'll take some." She hugged the blanket to her chest.

Joey went into his small kitchen and started the coffeemaker. While it brewed, he sat down in the armchair across from where Iris lay, admiring how good her tousled hair made her look in the early morning light. She must have sensed his thoughts, because she sat up and tried to smooth her hair.

"Did you grow up in SoCal?" he asked.

Iris looked like she might protest his questioning, but replied, "In Santa Ana. I'm living in my childhood home. So, I haven't gone far."

"That's nice," said Joey. "I had to move around a lot as a kid. What about your father? Where's he?"

"He passed away a few years ago. Heart attack and stroke that hit both at once. Mama was devastated."

"That's tough," Joey said, a sad look entering his eyes.

"You've been talking about your father in the past tense. I take it he also died?"

Joey nodded. "Bad ticker, too. What'd your father do?"

"He was an engineer, so he had a very analytical mind. When I told him I wanted to be a writer, we had a few debates about the likelihood of me making a decent living, but in the end, he agreed I should do what made me happy. What about you? What was your father like?"

"Pop was old-school blue collar. He drove a truck when I was young. Then when we moved to Orange County when I turned fifteen, he went to trade school to be an electrician. He was a hard ass in many ways, but he was always fair."

"It's hard to lose your father when he's been the rock of the family," Iris murmured.

That was a good way to put it, thought Joey. "My pop was my rock and anchor, that's for sure."

"I'm so grateful for my mother. I don't know what I'd do without her. She's really good with Jake," Iris said. "Did you ever try to find your mother?"

Joey thought about her words for a moment before answering. "I considered finding her a few times, but I didn't want to be disrespectful to Pop, you know? She never came to check up on me that I know of, so I figured she just forgot about me. He gave me a letter when I turned eighteen and said it would help me find her if I wanted to, but I never opened it. Let me get our coffee."

Once Joey returned with their steaming cups, he took a big spoonful of sugar from a bowl on the table and mixed it into his coffee. After a few sips, he set the cup down. "What I'm about to tell you is top secret. I shouldn't be telling you, but I don't see any other way out of this."

Iris waited.

"I'm not a gang member. I'm an undercover narcotics officer with the Santa Ana PD, and I infiltrated Raul's gang six months ago. My job is to figure out who is supplying black tar heroin to the streets of SoCal so we can shut the operation down. It's likely a Mexican cartel." Joey stopped talking and held his breath, waiting for Iris's reaction.

"Oh, thank God," she blurted out.

11

"I have to admit that you thanking God wasn't on my list of potential responses to the fact that I'm an undercover cop."

"I think it's better than you telling me that you're wanted in seven states."

"Just seven?" Joey smiled and studied her. "You really like being an investigative reporter?"

"So far, yes. Why?"

"I'm sure you need to check in at work. How about you tell your boss you need a few days to track down some leads on a story or something?"

"But then what?"

"I'm hoping I can blow this thing open in the next few days. If you help me, I can probably figure out who's running things from inside the *Recorder*. Then we'll haul in Raul and Ignacio, and you can go home to your son."

"How do you propose I help you, if I can't go into the paper?"

"You can make phone calls. You must have contacts. What about your partner, the one who was fired? You trust him?"

"I imagine he's not really pleased with me right now, given the fact that he was at the paper for thirty years, and I've only been there for five."

"I doubt he blames you," said Joey. "Call and feel him out."

Iris thought about Joey's request. She really missed talking to Henry. He'd taught her so much about investigative journalism, and journalism in general. She took a drink of coffee. "Okay. I'll tell my boss I need time to track down some leads on the slumlord article, and I'll call Henry."

Joey nodded in approval. "I've got an informant with a girlfriend who's a hacking whiz. She can get into the financials at the *Recorder.* You know the publisher?"

"I've seen him, but I haven't been formally introduced."

Joey got on his cellphone and made a call. "Twitch, it's me. Sammy around? TMI, man. Just let me talk to her."

Joey waited a moment. "Hey, Sammy, I've got another cyber job for you. Let's meet at the same place. Say, in an hour. I'm going to bring someone. I want you to work with her. Tell Twitch to stop whining about getting out of bed. I'll make it worth his while like I always do."

"Sammy is the cyber expert?" Iris asked once Joey hung up.

"Yeah. I've known Twitch for a few years. He hooked up with Sammy last year. He's always been helpful in terms of cluing me in to what's happening on the streets, and her cyber skills are incredible."

"What are you proposing I do about not being seen when we go out?"

Joey chuckled. "We're going to a place I'm pretty sure Raul and his boys don't frequent. The public library."

"I don't suppose you have a change of clothes for me?"

"No women's clothing here," Joey said, which gave Iris a small flutter in the pit of her stomach. "But you can borrow a t-shirt. It'll be a little big."

"I'll take it."

"I'll show you where the clean towels and stuff are, and there's a trick to turning on the shower."

Iris followed him into the bathroom, her heart rate picking up when they both stood inches from one another in the small space. She looked at his hair and wondered what it would feel like to run her fingers through it.

Joey opened a small cabinet and pointed to the towels. "There's soap and shampoo in the shower, and you need to pull up on the handle in order to turn it on."

"Thank you," said Iris, her heart skipping beats at this point. Then she realized her assumptions might be off. "Is this your only apartment?" she asked before thinking.

Joey's eyebrows raised. "You mean, do I have another place I live?"

Iris's vocal cords seemed to have frozen again, so she could only nod.

"This is my only place. And Raul has no idea where I live, if that's what you're worried about."

Iris found her voice. "Just curious."

She was relieved when he didn't seem to understand her real reason for the question, but then he asked, "What else you curious about?" A slight smiled played at the corners of his mouth, and his breath smelled like coffee. Normally, that would turn Iris off, but on Joey it was sexy. On him just about anything was sexy.

Joey's pulse heated up in the tight space of the bathroom. How he wanted to kiss Iris and not stop there. But he didn't trust himself to get into a relationship just yet. It'd only been fifteen months of sobriety for Joey, and sometimes it seemed like a week. Besides, if she knew about Joey's problem, she'd probably run the other way screaming. He would if he was her.

Joey backed out of the bathroom. "We've got to get going. I'll let you shower."

As Iris scrubbed her hair more vigorously than usual, she realized she was irritated. Why didn't Joey kiss her? She could sense that he wanted to. Granted, this was not the best time to start something. They had a lot to do, and a kiss or more would complicate things. By the time she had rinsed off and toweled dry, she had convinced herself this was for the best. She put on the t-shirt he had given her and tucked it into her pants, then walked out determined to keep things as professional as possible.

"Smells good," she said at the scent of bacon and eggs. "I'm starving."

"Raul called. He's all worked up about something. I'm going to take a quick shower, then drop you at the library and check in with him."

Iris suddenly lost her appetite. "I hope he doesn't decide to make a once in a lifetime run to the library today."

"I'll take care of him. You'll be fine." Joey went to the bathroom where the shower soon turned on. She sat down and forced herself to eat, refusing to think about the fact that this could be her last meal.

12

They walked into the Tustin Library, a hushed building on an out-of-the-way street, and headed to a study area on the second floor. A lanky young woman with straw-colored hair and wire-rimmed glasses sat at a table inches from a guy wearing a lime green shirt and biting his nails. The two stood up at the same time when she and Joey approached.

The man eyed her warily, but the woman stuck out her hand and smiled. "I'm Samantha, but everyone calls me Sammy." She elbowed Twitch in the side as he pulled away, sat down and stood up again. "This here is Twitch, my lesser half. He's real antsy. Just ignore him."

"I'm Iris. Nice to meet you both."

Sammy and Twitch took a seat, and Iris followed.

Joey stayed standing. "Twitch, Sammy, thanks for this," he told them. "I'll be back for Iris in about an hour. Hopefully you guys can get us some good info."

"You betcha," said Sammy, who opened her laptop as Joey walked away. "Did you bring the corn nuts?" she asked Twitch.

He reached into his pocket and pulled out a packet, plopping it on the table. "You're not supposed to eat in here," he said.

"He says, as I break, I don't know how many laws with my computer." Sammy eyed Iris. "Tell me what we're looking for."

Iris leaned closer to Sammy and quietly instructed her to dig into the financials at the *Recorder*, especially any large cash transactions.

"No problem." The girl picked up her corn nuts. "Want some?"

Iris shook her head, suddenly realizing that she hadn't yet talked to Leonard about work today. "I'm going to the bathroom for a minute."

Sammy didn't look up, but nodded, while Twitch opened the corn nuts and took a mouthful and began to crunch them.

In the bathroom, which was thankfully empty, Iris made the call to Leonard. She got his voicemail. "Hey, Leonard. I'm chasing a lead on the slumlord piece. I need to quote the owner, but I haven't been able to track him down. Sounds like he's holed up in Los Angeles, so I'm going there to pin him down. I'll keep you posted."

That done, she texted her mother to say she was doing fine. Then she headed back out to find Sammy looking rather animated.

"We've got some interesting stuff here," she said in a loud whisper.

Iris went to Sammy's side of the table and sat down next to her.

"I got into the general fund, for starters, and look at this." Sammy pointed. "For the last six months, every Friday, this cash infusion comes in." The number on the screen made Iris do a doubletake.

"Does that say what I think it says?"

"Sixty million. And that's likely just scratching the surface. Let me dig some more."

Iris sat back in her chair and watched as Sammy's fingers flew over the keyboard. The *Recorder* wasn't making that kind of money selling newspapers, which could only mean one thing. The publisher was involved with the drugs.

After another half-hour, Sammy came up with more damning evidence, including what appeared to be an offshore account where the sixty million deposited once a week. When Sammy finished, Iris asked, "Did you go to school to learn all that? I mean, I know hacking isn't taught specifically, but did you go to computer school?"

Sammy laughed. "No, my dad taught me everything I know. He was a computer hacker, too."

Just then Joey came rushing up. "I gotta get you back to my house. Sammy, get anything?"

"Yes, more than enough."

"Take care," Iris said, while Joey slipped a stack of bills to Twitch.

As Joey guided Iris out of the library, she sensed a nervous energy she hadn't picked up on him before. They headed for Joey's jeep and she asked, "Is anything wrong?"

"Plenty, but I don't want to get into it until we get to my place."

A few minutes later, back in Joey's apartment, Iris turned to him. "Does Raul know I'm alive?"

"Fortunately, you're not on his radar right now. He wants me to shoot Ignacio and grab the heroin when the drop is made tonight."

"Are they testing you, because of me last night? Because you didn't tell them about what you did with my body?"

Joey didn't answer. He sat down and began strumming his fingers on the coffee table. "You said you got something with Sammy?"

Iris filled him in, adding, "With the newspaper industry the way it is right now, the *Recorder* would be lucky to make sixty million in a year."

"So, we know it goes all the way to the top. It could be the publisher is planning to bail. Is there anyone you can call who could give you some insight on him? What's his name, anyway?"

"Antonio Ricci," said Iris. "Henry. I haven't called him yet. I was waiting to see what we dug up first."

"Go ahead and call him while I try to figure out what the hell I'm going to do about tonight."

Iris pulled out her phone and pressed speed dial. When Henry answered, his steady voice made her feel better instantly.

"Iris, so glad to hear from you. How is it going?"

"Okay, Henry, except for missing you."

"I'm hearing in your voice that's not the only reason you called me."

"You know me so well. Usually, I'd want to meet about this, but I'm pressed for time. It's an article I'm working on, but it's unsanctioned."

"You've gone rogue?"

Iris laughed. "Not by choice." Then she explained the circumstances of the last few days in broad strokes, ending with the recent information on the newspaper's finances.

"I'm not going to ask how you got that information, but that's explosive," Henry said.

"I was hoping you could give me some guidance."

"I would tell you to keep your nose out of things, but I know you won't do that, and frankly, neither would I," he said. "What I can tell you is about a rumor I heard about Antonio's father being a member of the Italian Mafia. Be extra careful, Iris."

13

Iris hung up the phone and sighed. "According to Henry, Antonio's father is probably Italian Mafia."

"I had a feeling given his last name. It's their MO. Infiltrate large companies, like the newspaper, with drug sales, and siphon the money into offshore accounts. A lot of those companies never recover."

Iris threw up her hands, stifling the urge to cry. "All I wanted was to be a journalist. Do you know how many people wanted to get a job at the *Recorder* from my graduating class? Practically everyone, and they only hired two of us."

Joey sat back in the armchair. "When did you start writing?"

The question centered Iris somewhat. "When I was six. My mother found me writing a story about a polar bear lost in the desert. She tells the story all the time."

Joey laughed. "She must be proud of you."

Iris smiled at how Joey shifted the conversation to something positive. She liked that.

"What about you? When did you decide you wanted to be a cop?"

"My journey is a little lengthier. Right now, we better figure out what to do about tonight."

Iris thought for a moment. "What if Ignacio doesn't make it to the meet?"

Joey leaned forward. "That could work, but it'd just prolong the inevitable."

"What if we could get Ignacio to talk, so you can tell your superiors and end this thing?"

"That would make my year. What do you propose?"

When Iris finished sharing her plan, Joey said levelly, "You sure you want to do this? It's dangerous and could tank your career at the *Recorder*."

"My prospects at the *Recorder* are worse if Antonio is left to drain the newspaper. Besides, I feel responsible for this mess. Raul wouldn't be ordering you to kill Ignacio if it wasn't for me."

When Iris told Ignacio to meet her at the apartment complex to take more photos, to her relief, he didn't question her. She told him Leonard had already sanctioned things and to meet her there right away.

Iris drove her Corolla, with Joey in the back seat. When they got to the apartment complex, Joey handed her a key. "Anything goes wrong, I want you to run back to my place. Stay there and wait to hear from me."

Iris slid the key into her pants pocket. When she saw Ignacio approaching, she stepped out of the car. Joey crouched down.

"Thanks for meeting me here," she said. "Let me just get my stuff."

When Iris pulled open the passenger side door, Joey had a gun trained on Ignacio. "Get in quietly, and you won't get hurt," he ordered.

As he climbed into the car, Ignacio asked Iris, "What the hell are you doing? You *loco*? And who the hell is he?"

When they arrived at their destination, a basement in a safehouse the Santa Ana PD used, Joey kept his gun trained on Ignacio while Iris duct taped him to a chair. She cringed when he glared at her, his eyes an inferno that had her wondering if this was a good idea, after all.

"Now that we're all settled, I'll answer your questions," she said to

Ignacio. "We know about the drugs you're hauling into the *Recorder*. And he's the man who's been ordered to kill you."

The anger in Ignacio's eyes turned to apprehension. "I don't know about any drugs."

"I saw you take the heroin from receiving the other night, and we know Antonio is Italian Mafia."

Ignacio looked from Iris to Joey and back again. Finally, he spoke. "If I talk, my family in Mexico is dead."

"If you don't talk, you're dead," said Iris.

"The Santa Ana PD can keep you safe," added Joey.

"What about my family?" Ignacio looked anxious and indecisive now.

"I have someone in the FBI I can call about that," Iris said quietly. Out of the corner of her eye, she saw a blip of surprise run across Joey's face.

"We can cover you and your family," Joey said. "We just need you to tell us what's going on."

Ignacio shook his head and muttered in Spanish. "I came here for a better life, so I could provide for my family in Mexico. I have a wife and son there, and *mi papa* and *mama*. I heard about the position at the *Recorder* through my professor back in Morelia. I was attending classes there and taking photos for a local newspaper, while also studying English. When I was told the position at the *Recorder* was in shipping and receiving, I didn't care. I was grateful to get a job *en Los Estados Unidos*. About six months after I got here, I was called to Antonio's office. He explained that my job was secure, and my family safe, as long as I picked up packages coming in on the loading dock at midnight. I was told not to open the packages and to put them in a utility room on the second floor."

"Are the packages gone when you go to put in more packages?" asked Joey.

"Yes. It was going along fine, until the other night when there was a shootout. I went to talk to Antonio afterwards. He said he would take care of things. That's all I know."

"Give us a minute," said Joey, pointing to a corner of the basement where he and Iris went to speak.

"I think he's telling the truth," Iris said.

"Me, too. We just need to get to the utility room before it's cleared out. I'll get the key from him and the room number. And I'll call the PD to get a cop to stand in for Ignacio tonight."

"What do you want me to do?"

"I want you to tell me who you know in the FBI." Joey's eyes bored into hers.

"My Aunt Joanna."

"What's her last name?"

"Molinaro."

"FBI San Diego?

"Do you know her?"

Joey looked uncomfortable. "Yes, I do."

14

"Did something happen between you and my Aunt?"

"That's not a conversation for right now. I'm going to call my handler and set things up for tonight."

As he took out his cellphone, Joey tried to hide the fact that his hands were shaking. The news about Iris's aunt had catapulted him to a time in his life that he would rather forget.

"I'm fine, Pop. Just let me get going."

"Hell, you're fine. You're all boozed up. You can't go to work. You could get yourself or someone else killed."

"I don't go, and a bunch of good people are in jeopardy."

His father stood with his arms crossed over his chest in front of the door. "You'll never find your keys."

That filled Joey with rage. "I'm not a kid anymore. You can't stop me from doing what I want to do. Is that what you did to mom? Is that why she left?"

As soon as the words left his mouth, Joey knew he'd hit a nerve that he shouldn't have and wished he could take the words back.

"Look, how about you drop me off near the meet. Will that work? I gotta be there. I don't think you understand."

"I served in the military. No man left behind. I understand. I also understand that when a man was compromised, I didn't want him watching my back."

"Give me some coffee, that'll help."

Joey's father's shoulders slumped. "Fine. Then I'll drive you."

He waited until he heard the coffee machine being filled before he took the keys to his pop's truck and left the house.

After Joey hung up the phone, he announced, "Someone from the PD is coming to stay here with you, Ignacio."

"What about my family?"

Joey looked to Iris. "That's the next call we're going to make."

"I'll call from the kitchen, if that's okay." Iris didn't wait for Joey to respond as she climbed the stairs and sat down at the kitchen table. She pushed the number for her Aunt Joanna and listened to it ring several times. "Molinaro."

"Aunt Joanna? It's Iris. Can you hear me?" Iris heard what sounded like wind on the other end of the phone.

"Iris! You okay? Sorry, I'm on a convoy right now."

"I'm fine, but I need your help. Someone needs protection."

"From what?"

"Some bad people. This is regarding a story I'm working on at the *Recorder*. When will you be coming back?"

"Not for a few days, but your Uncle Tony is at the San Diego Bureau now. Call him. You sure you're okay?"

"Yes, don't worry about me, *Tia*. You stay safe."

"You get ahold of her?" Iris jumped and swung around to see Joey standing right behind her.

"She's on assignment. She told me to call my Uncle Tony. He used to live in Mexico, but he works for the Bureau now." Iris watched Joey's tense face relax. "Are you going to tell me what happened with my aunt?"

"It wasn't my finest hour. Call your uncle."

By the time Iris hung up the phone, her uncle was fully briefed, and promised to call contacts in Mexico to help protect Ignacio's family. When the officer sent to guard Ignacio showed up at the safehouse, they informed him that his family was being guarded. "*Gracias a Dios,*" Ignacio said. He looked to Iris as if he was about to cry.

Back in the car, Iris asked, "What now?"

"I'll take you back to my house where you can wait until this thing is resolved tonight. Then I'll take you home to your mom and son."

After being in the eye of the storm for the last day or so, Joey's words deflated her. "But what about my story? How am I going to gather information for it if I'm holed up in your apartment?"

"I'll fill you in. Besides, I didn't know you were going to write about this. It could tank the newspaper altogether."

"The paper is going to have other problems if Antonio gets carted off to jail. I think telling the truth is the only thing that might save the paper."

When they arrived in front of Joey's apartment door, he glanced at Iris. She was about to ask him what he was waiting for when she remembered that he'd given her his key. "Oh, sorry," she said, pulling it from her pocket.

"It's been a long time since I gave a woman the key to my apartment." Joey turned the lock and pushed the door open, motioning for her to go in first.

They stopped in the entryway facing one another. "How long has it been?" Iris asked.

Joey moved closer, his breath on her cheek sending ripples of pleasure into her chest. "Too long to matter. What about you?"

"The last man to have a key to my place was my ex-husband."

They were inches from one another, and Iris didn't move, afraid to break the spell. Her breath quickened. "Is there something else you want to ask me?"

Joey reached out and pulled her to him. "Can I kiss you?" His words were almost a whisper.

Iris didn't answer but stared into his eyes. They were the darkest shade of brown and suddenly she felt glad to know how it was to want a man this much.

Joey leaned forward and touched his lips to hers, tentatively at first, then took her in his arms as he kissed her deeply and long. His tongue searched for hers, and she could feel the heat of his hands on her breasts through her blouse. She reached up and grasped the back of his neck, her body all soft and trembly. If this was a dream, she didn't want it to end.

Joey had heard about fireworks going off during a kiss but had never experienced it. Until now. He'd describe this as a bomb. He knew he had promised himself he wouldn't start something between them, but he felt lost to his desire for her. He began to gently guide her backwards toward his unmade bed with its wild tumble of sheets. And then his phone buzzed. "Dammit," he said, as he fumbled with one hand for his phone when it fell on the floor. Iris stepped back so he could pick up the phone. He reached down and checked the display as it started ringing again.

"You better get it," she said.

Joey nodded and answered. "Yeah?"

Iris went to the kitchen to get a glass of water while Joey talked on the phone. Both her hands grasped the edge of the sink as her mouth longed for his, her body aching with desire. She had to admit it was probably a good thing he got that phone call. This was no time to start whatever this was. She filled a tumbler with water and rolled the cold glass across her forehead, then pressed it against one cheek when Joey said, "That was Raul. They want me at the warehouse right away. The shipment has been moved up." Joey scanned her face. "You going to be okay?"

Iris set down the water glass. "I think that's something I should be asking you."

After he left the apartment, Iris went into the living room and sat down on the couch. She leaned back and gave a silent prayer that nothing would happen to him as she listened to his jeep pull away from the apartment complex. Just as she was starting to doze off, a cellphone buzzed. Iris shot up. Joey had forgotten his phone on the table. Right away, she grabbed it and checked the display. A text read: *Extract immediately. R knows.*

15

Iris gasped when she saw the message and thought about running outside to look for his car, but she knew Joey had already driven off. She grabbed her cellphone and called her Uncle Tony, but it went straight to voicemail. Hanging up, she racked her brain for who else to call.

Twitch! She had Sammy's number.

"Hi Sammy, it's Iris."

"How's it going?"

"Not so good. I need Twitch. Is he with you?"

She heard muffled voices.

"Twitch here."

"Where does Raul and his gang hang out?"

"Why?"

"I think Raul knows Joey's a cop. Where is the gang headquarters, or whatever you call it?"

"On Baker in Costa Mesa. 554. But you can't go there alone—"

Iris hung up and stuffed her and Joey's phones into her pants pocket. Grabbing her keys, she raced out the door. It would take her fifteen minutes to get from Tustin to Costa Mesa, if she floored it.

When she approached the address Twitch had given her, she parked a block away. After locking the car door, she walked quickly down the street.

The warehouse door was locked, but she could hear voices inside. Hurrying around to the back of the building, she found a dumpster wedged under a set of windows. She wasn't sure if she could get on top of the dumpster to see in through the glass, but she was going to try. Grasping the top edge of the metal bin, she used every muscle in her arms to hoist herself up the side of the dumpster and pull one leg over. Once she straddled the edge, she scooted to the side of the building. There were safety bars on the windows, which she reached out for, then swung her right leg up, carefully placing her foot on the side of the dumpster. She used her arms to pull her body and other leg up. Pulse pounding in her ears, she balanced precariously and peered inside.

Two men had their guns trained on Joey, and another one screamed obscenities inches from his face. She needed to create a distraction. Glancing down into the dumpster, she saw a steel pole. Holding on with one hand, she reached in and grabbed it, then smashed one end into the window as hard as she could. An entire pane busted and shattered to the floor. Everyone glanced up, giving Joey a chance to pull his gun and shoot the two men. Holding his gun on Raul then, Joey backed out of the building.

Adrenaline moving her forward, Iris tried to walk the edge of the dumpster so she could jump off but ended up sliding inside. Recoiling as her feet sank into something soft and slippery, she scrabbled to try to climb up the inside of the dumpster walls. Just then, Joey appeared at the top of the dumpster and reached down, pulling her up by the armpits, then up and over and onto the sidewalk.

They took off towards the street. As they neared Joey's jeep, a shot rang out, bursting one of the tires. The jeep responded by tilting to one side.

"My car is up ahead," Iris cried.

"Stay in front of me," he ordered.

They ran several yards when Iris heard someone shouting behind them. "You think you can run, narc! I'll find you. You're both *muerto!*"

Iris hopped in the driver's seat while Joey got in the passenger side, and yelled, "Drive!"

As the car careened into traffic, a bullet came crashing through the back window, embedding itself in her dashboard.

Joey fired back through the broken window, the sound ricocheting off the asphalt. "He's on foot. There's no way he's going to catch us."

Once she had driven several blocks, Joey cried, "What in the hell were you thinking?"

"What was I thinking? I saved you. And don't tell me you had it handled." Iris dug in her pants pocket and threw Joey's phone at him. "Check the last text."

Joey stared at the display. "Shit."

"Shit is right. From where I sit, you were one bullet away from dead."

Joey had no idea how things had gone sideways so fast. His heart still hammered in his chest.

As Iris pulled into his apartment complex and turned off the car, he said, "Thank you."

"You're welcome."

Joey ran his hands through his hair and thought how good a drink would feel right now. He shook the thought out of his head.

"We gotta hide your car," he said. Joey started to dial Twitch's number, then stopped. "Is Twitch how you found me?"

"Don't get mad at him. He told me not to go. And if he hadn't helped," Iris reached out her hand and put it over Joey's. His hand was hot and clammy under her touch, the tenseness in his body releasing slightly as if her caress seemed to calm him down a notch. "You'd be dead right now."

Joey paused, then dialed Twitch's number. When his informant answered tentatively, Joey took a deep breath and said, "It's me."

"Thank God! Iris found you in time?"

"Yes, but we're in deep shit now. My jeep had a blowout, and Iris's car is at my place. Can you come get her car and store it at your house? I'll have the PD tow my jeep."

"I'll come right now. I'm glad you're okay, man."

Joey hung up as Iris got out and headed toward his apartment. As he followed behind her, a feeling he'd never had before filled his chest. Overwhelming gratitude.

16

Once they walked into Joey's quiet apartment, he could tell by the expression on Iris's face that the reality of what just happened was beginning to sink in.

"Now what are we going to do?" she asked as he closed and bolted his apartment door.

Without answering, he took a step toward her and pulled her to him, his chest felt warm and solid against hers. He held her like that for a while, his heart beating fast, then slower and steadier, until their heartbeats kept pace with one another. Finally, he whispered into her hair, "I'm so glad you're okay."

Iris pulled back and gazed into his eyes. But before she could respond, his phone rang. He checked the caller ID and answered.

"Landau, you okay?" asked Bennett, his handler at the PD.

"I'm fine."

"We're putting you on something else. The boss wants you to come in and debrief."

Joey didn't say anything.

"Landau. You there?"

"We've got a problem," Joey said. "There was a civilian involved. She's in danger."

"How the hell did that happen?"

"It's a long story. Just let me finish this. Right now, all you have is a thug drug dealer, who doesn't know anything about the source of the heroin. He was just trying to intercept it."

Joey waited while Bennett weighed his words.

"I'll talk to the chief. Bring the civilian in. We'll make sure he or she stays safe."

"She's got a family."

"We'll put her family into protective custody right now."

Joey sighed. Bennett was right. Until this was resolved, Iris and her son and mother needed protection.

"What's the address at your place?" Joey asked Iris. "The PD needs to pick up your mom and son and place them in protective custody."

Iris sat up. "What! That will scare my son and totally disrupt their lives."

"You'll be with them," Joey explained.

"But I have a job to do, which is to report on what just happened."

"Bennett, can I call you back?" asked Joey.

When he hung up, he looked at Iris. "I know this sucks, but it's the only way to keep you all safe."

"I won't do it. My mom and Jake can go, but I'm not going." Iris folded her arms.

"You're a civilian."

"I am a journalist. And this is just as much my story as it is your case. They can't force me to go into protective custody, can they?" She studied Joey's face. "That's what I thought. They can't."

"They can arrest you for obstructing justice."

Iris bolted up from where she sat on the couch. "You wouldn't dare!"

"To keep you safe, I would."

Iris reached for her keys on the coffee table.

"What are you doing?"

She headed for the door and was just about to open it, when there was a knock. Joey sprang up behind her and leaned around her to peer through the peephole. Then he pulled the door open.

Twitch stood in the doorway, shifting from one foot to the other. "You got the keys? It's the yellow Corolla, right?"

"Yes," said Iris, handing him the car keys. "It should have enough gas to get you to Long Beach."

Twitch nodded as Joey handed him some cash.

Once Twitch left, Iris said, "I'll give you the address to my house, and I'll call my mom and Jake, but I refuse to sit on my hands in protective custody."

"I'll take that," said Joey. "Use my burner phone to call them."

"Iris? Where are you?"

"Hi Mama. I'm fine but listen carefully. You and Jake are going to be put into protective custody. It's because of a story I'm working on. You could be in danger. I need you to pack bags right away."

"*Dios mio! Qué pasa, hija?*"

"I don't have time to go into it right now. Just be ready for two Santa Ana police officers to come and get you very soon. I'll check in later."

"*Ay*, okay. When will we be able to return home?"

"I'm sorry, Mama, I don't know. Please kiss Jake for me and tell him I love him. I'll contact you as soon as I'm able. It's going to be okay."

"I sure hope so, *hija*. You're all Jake has in this world."

Iris fought back tears. "He has you, Mama. And I trust you implicitly with him. *Te quiero mucho.* I have to go."

Joey took the phone back and asked quietly, "You sure about this? You won't be any less of a person if you decide to be with your mother and son."

"I'm sure. Now that I know Jake and my mama are going to be okay.'"

Iris gave him their address and listened as he called his handler. She could hear a woman's loud and displeased voice on the other end of the line when he told her that Iris refused protective custody. Then he hung up, worry in his eyes.

"I'm sorry," said Iris. "I know I'm putting you in a tight spot, but if you were me, you wouldn't go into protective custody, either."

Joey sat down on the couch and eyed the ceiling. "You're right. And you don't need to keep apologizing. This is my mess. You just got pulled into it."

Iris's phone buzzed. She eyed the display. "It's Henry."

"Does he know what's going on?"

"Only broad strokes."

"Go ahead," said Joey. "But don't stay on long. And turn it off when you're done, so it can't be tracked."

Iris nodded and answered. "Henry."

"Iris. So glad I caught you. Word is Antonio is flying out tomorrow morning, to Italy."

"Do you know details?"

"Six a.m. flight to Rome. LAX."

"I owe you one."

"Iris, be careful. I hope you have backup."

Iris glanced at Joey, who watched her intently. "I do."

Henry was quiet.

"Anything else?"

"I never told you this," he said. "You have the makings of a fine investigative journalist. Just don't go and get yourself killed."

Iris smiled. "Now that I have that to live up to, Henry, I can't."

17

Iris hung up the phone and filled Joey in.

"We better start packing," he said. "We can check into a hotel near the airport."

"We?"

"I'm not leaving you behind. The PD is taking Raul into custody, but he's got guys everywhere."

"I need to get my passport from my house," Iris said.

"We'll go there next."

Joey ran to the small closet near his bed and pulled out his go bag. He unzipped it and checked the contents. A few bags of pistachios, along with several changes of clothing, toiletry items and his passport. He threw in his leather jacket, then made one final sweep of his bedroom area. His eye fell on the wooden box on his dresser. He went over and took out the envelope that lay at the bottom and slid it into his bag.

"Looks like you're all set," said Iris. "Just one problem. We have no car."

"Oh, shit." Joey pulled out his cellphone and dialed Twitch.

"I'll be home in about ten minutes. I don't think anyone followed me."

"That's great," said Joey. "When you drop off Iris's car, can you come back and take us to a hotel near LAX?"

"You shitting me! Sammy and I were going to a meeting."

"Sorry, bro, but I don't have any wheels right now. And they have AA meetings 24/7 here in OC. You can catch one after."

"Fine," Twitch grumbled. "We'll be there in a half hour or so."

"I didn't realize they had AA meetings 24/7 in Orange County," said Iris when Joey hung up the phone.

"Maybe not 24/7 but pretty close."

"Do they?" She turned to look at him.

Joey went into the kitchen. "You want a snack while we wait?" He didn't want to have a conversation about his alcohol problem just yet. He wasn't the same guy who walked into an AA meeting fifteen months ago after hitting rock bottom and almost offing himself. "You might want to check in with your mom and Jake. Make sure they got settled at the safehouse okay." Joey pulled out some tortilla strips and a bottle of salsa from the refrigerator. "Use my phone." He walked over with the chips and salsa in one hand and his phone in the other. When Iris took the phone from his hand without saying a word and dialed her mother, he realized he'd been holding his breath, expecting more questions about AA. Plopping the bag of strips on the table and the jar of salsa, he sat down and took a handful.

As Iris talked to her mother and Jake, Joey snuck glances at her. He noticed how her face softened when she talked to her son. A couple of times, it looked like she was about to cry. When she sang Jake a little nursery rhyme in Spanish, Joey felt choked up himself. Whatever the hell was happening between them, he wasn't so sure he minded.

Iris watched Joey scarf down chips and salsa while she talked to Jake. Her son was old enough to know that being guarded by the police in a secret house was a serious matter, so it took Iris awhile to calm him down and assure him that all would be okay. As she made promises, Iris prayed that she would keep them.

When she hung up, she reached for the bag of tortilla strips. "I guess this is dinner?"

Joey shrugged. "We can order room service when we get to the hotel."

Iris must have looked uncomfortable, because he added, "Did you want two rooms?"

Iris reddened. "No, I—. I mean it's fine if…"

Joey laughed and leaned back on the couch. He put his hands behind his head as Iris found herself squirming under his gaze.

"One room is fine," she said. "It's not like we're going to be doing all that much sleeping. I mean we won't be there long." She was digging herself in deeper and deeper.

Joey chuckled. "I know what you meant."

Iris was grateful to end the conversation when someone rapped on the door. Joey went to see who it was; then announced, "You ready?"

Gathering as much of her dignity as possible, Iris rose from the couch and walked out the door with him.

"Cool car," said Joey, as they approached a turquoise VW Bug.

"Thanks, it's mine," said Sammy, who wore her hair in Pippy-style ponytails today. "Pile in." She headed for the driver's seat.

"I can drive," said Twitch.

Sammy ignored him and got behind a fuzzy pink steering wheel. As she fired the car to life, Twitch turned around and said, "She's a crazy driver. Watch out. And she tailgates."

Iris laughed. "Thanks, but I think her driving is going to be tame compared to what we're up against."

"Speaking of that. Word is the most recent batch of black tar heroin is especially potent," said Twitch. "There's been a lot more overdoses in the last few days."

Joey shook his head. "Hopefully we can get to the bottom of this when we're in Italy and stop the flow."

"I never been to Italy, but I hear it's nice," said Sammy.

"Yeah, me neither," Iris heard Joey murmur. Considering that Joey's mother was from Italy, Iris thought it interesting that he'd never been there.

After Iris grabbed her things from her house, they made their way to a hotel near LAX. When they neared their destination, Twitch and Sammy began debating about who should drive home.

"How about you drop us off in front of the hotel and continue your lover's quarrel once we get out," Joey suggested.

Sammy pulled up in front of the hotel's lobby and turned back to them, a grin on her face. "Sorry about Mr. Grumpy Pants. He's mad we missed the AA meeting with the Krispy Kreme Donuts."

Twitch snorted while Joey handed Sammy a wad of cash. "You guys divvy this up. Buy yourselves a bunch of donuts when you get home."

As he and Iris trudged through the sliding glass doors of the hotel and into the cool, quiet lobby, Iris suddenly felt a flattening fatigue and couldn't wait to drop into bed. When they were a few feet from the reception desk, she was about to ask Joey if he was tired, too, when she caught someone familiar out of the corner of her eye. Not knowing what to do, she swung around and embraced Joey.

"I take it you don't want two rooms?" He grinned.

Iris leaned in, pretending to nibble his ear and whispered, "Don't look now, but Antonio is behind us."

18

Joey peered over Iris's shoulder to see a tall guy in an expensive black suit. He had a suitcase and leather computer bag with him.

"I told you not to look," Iris hissed.

"He's never seen me before. You think he'll remember you?"

"I don't want to take the chance."

"Thank you, Mr. Rossi," said the woman at the front desk to Antonio. "The elevators are right over there." Joey watched as Antonio walked away.

"You sure that's him?" he whispered.

"I'm positive, but he's not using his real last name. It's Ricci."

"Hello, checking in?" The woman standing at attention behind the desk gave them a broad smile.

"We don't have a reservation, but yes, we'd like a room for one night," said Joey as they approached the front desk.

The receptionist nodded and began typing away on the computer. "We have a room on the eighth floor on the south side of the building."

"Perfect." Joey handed her a credit card.

"Thank you, Mr. Sandolf. Let me get you checked in."

Iris raised an eyebrow when the receptionist announced his alias. Joey grinned. She liked their easy camaraderie.

"Ready, Mrs. Sandolf?" Joey broke into her reverie. "Our room awaits."

Iris motioned to pick up her bag, but Joey beat her to it. She was about to protest, but then admitted to herself that Joey had enough muscles to carry ten suitcases. She followed him toward the elevators.

When they got inside and Joey pressed their floor, Iris yawned.

"I'm beat, too," he said, pulling out his cellphone and checking the time. "It's nearly eleven o'clock. We need to be at LAX by four a.m. That doesn't give us much time to sleep, but it'll help."

"Wait, what about plane tickets?" Iris suddenly realized.

"All covered," said Joey. "I bought them while we were in the car. I'll get reimbursed by the PD. Somehow."

"That doesn't sound that promising," said Iris as they exited the elevator and made their way down the carpeted hallway.

"If I bring Antonio back to the states and stop the heroin flooding Santa Ana, the PD will happily pay for all my expenses."

"Is that how it works? That seems odd." Iris watched as Joey put the keycard into the lock and the green light turned on.

"No, not exactly." He pushed the door open and motioned for her to go inside.

Iris stayed in the hallway. "What does that mean?"

"Go in, and I'll tell you," said Joey.

Iris walked inside and turned on the light as Joey set down the luggage on the bed. Then he turned to her. "The PD doesn't know I'm going after Antonio in Italy. I just told them I had a lead, and I'd be in touch."

"So, we don't have any backup? It's just you and me?"

"For now. I have a few international sources I can tap. We'll be fine. Besides, you didn't get this okayed at the paper."

He had a point. "I could call my Aunt Joanna."

"No, don't." Joey went to the refrigerator and checked the contents.

"What happened with you and my aunt?"

"They've got some sodas in here."

Iris walked up behind Joey and waited. Finally, Joey sighed and turned around to face her. "Let's just say, she saw me at my worst. I'm not proud of that time in my life. I got shot and almost died. My Pop died." The pain in Joey's eyes when he mentioned his father was palatable. "If you want to know, I'll tell you."

She shook her head. "It'll keep. We should get some sleep."

Iris took the bathroom first to prepare for bed. Nervous about what this night might bring, she'd packed a knee-length gown. When she emerged, Joey was in shorts already. "I can sleep on the floor, no problem," he said.

Iris slid between the sheets. "Don't be silly."

After he used the bathroom, Joey climbed into bed with her. Soon after, his comforting presence lulled Iris to sleep.

Joey lay in bed, trying to slow down his mind. He was glad she hadn't insisted he tell her about what happened with her Aunt Joanna. He dreaded the look of disappointment and maybe even disdain in her eyes. He'd learned in AA that it was best to come clean about what he did when he was drinking. But he was another person back then. Whenever he looked back on that one horrible night, it felt like he was watching some terrible flick about someone else.

Pop didn't understand, Joey thought as he floored it in the old truck. He had to get to the meet. The FBI would be there tonight, so he had to do this right. He probably shouldn't have had those beers, but truth was, he was nervous. He had to make a good impression.

When he got close to the location for the exchange, he fished around in the glove compartment for a mint. Nothing. He pulled into the parking lot and shut off the truck engine, getting out and slamming the door.

"*Hijole, hombre,* you think you made enough noise with the clunker? And what'd you do, man, take a bath in beer?" asked Pedro.

"I'm here, aren't I?" said Joey. "Where's my girl?"

"She's waiting for the Ukrainians. You better get over there. She's been looking for you."

Just then a black town car pulled in and headed toward where Dawn waited. Joey hurried over as two men got out of the car. Damnit, it was hard to make them out. Did they have guns?

Iris woke up to Joey jerking about in bed. When he shouted out, "Don't shoot!" she grabbed his arm and shook it. "Joey, you're having a bad dream." It took several shakes before he stopped thrashing about and yelling. She watched as he blinked and slowly became conscious.

"Was I snoring or something?" he said.

"You were shouting." She put her hand on his chest to calm his wildly beating heart.

Joey ran his hands over his face. "Sorry I woke you up."

Iris kept her hand on his chest. Then she pushed herself up on one elbow and studied his face. Finally, the tightness in his brow relaxed.

Joey felt hypnotized as he watched her above him. She looked so beautiful in the light filtering through the window coverings from the street lamps. When the tips of her hair brushed over his chest, desire burned to his marrow. He closed his eyes for a moment, trying to quiet his hunger for her. Then he took her hand and kissed each of her fingertips, lingering on one and then another, staring into her eyes. She took a long, soft breath and raised her arms to lift her nightgown over her head, then leaned down and pressed herself against him. The feel of her warm skin on his brought a lump of emotion to Joey's throat. As he raised up to take her in his arms, something clutched in his chest. He asked himself, did he deserve her?

19

What was it about Joey that so intrigued her? She had surprised herself taking off her nightgown. She'd never done anything like that before, but there was a wild button that Joey pushed inside of her, and she liked it.

A shiver trembled through Iris as he watched her naked. He had such an earnest way of looking at her. Not like guys who feasted on her with their eyes. It was as if he wanted to see inside her, allowing him her every thought. To see what she cared about most.

"You sure about this?" Joey asked. "I don't want to pressure you."

Iris laughed. "I'm the one who took off my nightgown."

The tension slid out of Joey's eyes then, and, like a slow-moving fire, desire overtook them. He pulled her toward him, his tongue whispering across her skin, down her neck and between her breasts, making her feel trusting and fragile. She knew how much he wanted her, and the very thought sent a rush of heat throughout her body. She didn't say a word as he eased her back on the bed and his tongue made its way down her belly, exploring her most sensual parts as she gripped handfuls of the sheets and gasped, calling out his name in order to hear it on her own lips.

He held back then, and taking his time, ran his hands over her legs and stomach, her breasts and shoulders. He turned her over and felt the smooth roundness of her buttocks. Then turned her back. She waited, breathless, unsure of what he'd do next. Then, he lowered his head and took her in his mouth again, sweet and pure, teasing her with his tongue, until she was just about to climax, and she cried out, "Don't stop…please, Joey." At the crest of the most impassioned moment she had ever felt, he held her there, and tears suddenly flowed from her. What she felt with Joey was so intense and deep it seemed as if she had never made love with a man before this.

Joey straddled and entered Iris, slowly at first, until the world seemed to rock between them, exploding in his body, colors filling his brain. Maybe it was foolish, but all Joey had wanted was to be the best Iris had ever had. He had been willing to sacrifice everything for that. But their emotions and physical passion rode so high that Joey believed her tears and afterward buried his face in her hair, wishing the moment between them would never end.

"That was like every wish I ever had coming true," Joey said, his words muffled against her neck.

"I didn't know it could be like that," Iris breathed, holding him close.

Iris woke and panicked for a moment, until she saw that it was still dark. She flopped back down, relieved they hadn't slept until morning and missed the plane. Reaching out to the other side of the bed, she expected to find Joey, but her hand hit the cool mattress.

"It's almost 3:30," said his voice. "We need to get going soon." Joey sat in the darkened room at the nearby table.

Iris smelled coffee and asked, "Did you get any sleep?"

"Some. You?"

"Yes, after…" Iris trailed off, feeling herself blush.

Joey laughed. "For a journalist, you sure have a way with words."

"Do I smell coffee?"

"Of course."

Iris sat up and reached for her nightgown.

"Don't," said Joey.

She slid out of bed and padded naked over to him. He wore shorts, his chest bare.

"Where am I supposed to sit?" She pointed to the only other chair, piled with Joey's belongings.

He patted his lap. "Right here. I've got your coffee. Come drink it."

Iris smiled and slid onto his lap. The feel of his tight, muscular body under her bare bottom sent a ripple of desire through her. Picking up the full coffee cup next to him, she took a tentative sip. "Perfect," she murmured.

"Not as perfect as you." Joey ran his tongue along the back of her left shoulder. "Don't worry, I'm not starting anything. After we finish our coffees, we need to get out of here."

They arrived at LAX in plenty of time to get through security and find a seat near the gate. Joey went to the sundry stand while Iris stayed behind and kept an eye out for Antonio.

"Don't look now, but he's just over there," said Joey when he returned and handed her an icy cold water and a pack of chewing gum.

Iris took a quick glance and saw Antonio busy typing on his laptop as the gate agent announced boarding for first-class passengers. Before long, they began the boarding process. Iris was relieved to see that Antonio was in the first group to get on the plane.

"I guess I should be glad he spent the newspaper's money on first-class tickets," said Iris. "Makes it less likely that we'll run into him in coach."

"You're forgetting one thing. We have to walk through first class to get to coach."

Iris groaned. A few minutes later, they got stuck in first class waiting for passengers up ahead to stow their carry-ons. Antonio was seated facing the oncoming passengers, but he was working on his computer.

She tried to remain calm as they inched along and was just about ready to pass him when his eyes flew up from his computer to meet hers.

He quickly checked out her face. "Do I know you?"

Her heart thudding in her brain, Iris couldn't think of what to say. If she refused to speak, that would look suspicious.

Joey was behind her. He reached in front of her and did what appeared to be sign language, directed at her.

Iris knew absolutely no sign language, so she shook her head.

"She's deaf," Joey explained as they passed Antonio. "But she said she's never seen you before."

"Forgive my intrusion," said Antonio. He glanced out the window, but Iris could see a confused furrow in his brow.

When they found their seats and sank into them, Joey pulled out a big bag of pistachios.

"Smart move with Antonio," she said, reaching for a handful of nuts.

"Thank you." Joey leaned over and gave her a quick kiss, surprising Iris. She thought of the intimate hours they'd shared earlier and realized she was probably blushing again.

As they took off, she felt excited about what lay ahead. Iris switched from nuts to gum to keep her ears from popping. She glanced at Joey. He had started to nod off, leaning against the window. She had a feeling he hadn't slept much at all last night.

After the plane leveled off and the captain said they could move about the cabin, Iris contemplated getting out her computer to work when someone appeared in the aisle next to her seat.

"I remembered where I've seen you before." It was Antonio.

20

Iris thought about shaking Joey awake. Instead, she just smiled.

"You're a teacher at the Braille Institute in Anaheim where my niece teaches."

Iris nodded and continued to smile.

"I guess you read lips. I didn't realize that the teachers there were also deaf, but I guess that makes sense. Well, anyway, I just wanted to let you know that I remembered." Antonio eyed Joey. "Sorry to bother you."

Iris nodded and then made the okay sign, and Antonio went back to his seat.

"What the hell was that all about?" Joey spoke, his eyes still closed.

"I don't know." Iris whispered.

"Well, we need to stop talking to each other for the duration of the flight."

"Great," Iris grumbled. "You can order my meal. I want the chicken plate."

Joey opened his eyes and stretched. "Great nap," he commented.

"It's clear who's going to have a hard time with let's not talk to each other."

Joey leaned over and kissed the side of Iris's neck, murmuring in her ear. "No need to talk when there's so much else we could be doing."

. . .

At their layover in New York City several hours later, Iris managed to not run into Antonio as they exited the plane. In the bathroom at JFK Airport, she checked her reflection in the mirror. There were dark circles under her eyes, but she noted a spark in them she'd rarely seen before.

Joey was waiting for her outside of the bathroom. "I saw our boy in a bar down the way. Looks like he's doing a bit of drinking."

"I smelled alcohol on him when he talked to me on the plane."

"Maybe we can take advantage of his loose tongue. Let's go talk to Antonio."

"What if he figures out who I am?"

"Either he already has, or he really thinks you're from the Braille Institute. Let's see what else we can get out of him." Joey started walking. Iris hesitated before catching up.

Joey walked up to the bar next to Antonio and asked the bartender, "Can I get a club soda with lime and a V-8, if you have one?"

"Hey, it's you," Antonio called out. Joey noticed a slur in his words. He turned, purposely registering surprise in his eyes.

"You were on our flight. How's it going?" Joey sat down next to Antonio and motioned for Iris to sit next to him. "This will be me and my wife's first time to Rome," Joey added. "Any suggestions on where to visit when we're there?"

Antonio drained his drink, plunking the glass down. "Another whiskey sour, please." He turned to Joey, his eyes taking on the glassy sheen Joey knew so well. "I'd say see everything, but you probably don't have time for that. Start out with the Sistene Chapel. Make sure to eat at Napoloti Restaurant. Where you staying?"

"Shoot. I'm trying to remember the name. I think it's starts with S."

"St. Regis?" Antonio took a slug of the new drink the bartender set in front of him.

"Yes, I think so." Joey turned to Iris and made some hand gestures. She nodded in reply.

"That's it. Is it a good hotel?"

"Excellent. And it just so happens that's where I'm staying."

"Oh, you're not from Rome? I thought you might be going home."

Antonio sighed, moving his glass in a circular motion on the bar. "I was born and raised in Rome, but I've spent the last two decades in California. I might be staying there, though."

"Oh?"

"Yes, indefinitely."

"I hear you, man. I've made a few mistakes along the way and had to bail myself." Joey held his breath. He figured Antonio was shrewd and might pick up on his over interest, but he was banking on him not noticing, considering how inebriated he was.

Antonio swirled the ice cubes in his glass. "You'd think after all these years, I would have learned," he said, almost to himself. "But I never learn. And now I could lose everything."

"Sounds pretty heavy, man." Joey said quietly.

"I've always told them that I didn't want any part of this, but my father..." Antonio was mumbling and blinking as if to focus his eyes.

"Who doesn't have dad issues?" said Joey, hoping he would continue. Suddenly, the loudspeaker announced that their flight was boarding.

"We better get going." The announcement woke Antonio from his stupor. He stood and took out his wallet, removing a one-hundred-dollar bill and waving it at the bartender. "I'm paying for theirs, too. No change needed." Then he headed out of the bar toward the gate, nearly knocking down a woman and her little boy in the process.

21

"We better make sure he gets on the plane," said Joey, who grabbed both bags in one hand as if they were filled with feathers.

"Did you play football in high school or something?" Iris asked as they hurried to the gate.

"No. I box."

That surprised Iris. "Box. As in present tense?"

Joey nodded, then slowed, motioning with his head to a few yards in front of them where Antonio stood at the front of the line, weaving from one side to the other.

"Stay here in line with the bags." He put them at Iris's feet. "I'm going to go ingratiate myself."

Joey came up behind Antonio, who struggled to get his wallet open with one hand, while holding onto his carry-on bag, as his laptop appeared to be slipping out of his grasp.

"Hey, buddy," Joey said. "Need some help?"

Antonio turned, recognition flashing in his eyes. "Hey, it's you."

"How about I hold a couple of things for you?"

Antonio gratefully piled his bag and computer into Joey's arms, but still grappled to remove his license.

"Do you know him?" asked the ticket agent.

"Yes, my boss," Joey mouthed. "He's really nervous about flying. If I can just help get him into his seat, he'll fall asleep."

The ticketing agent picked up a phone and pressed a button, putting the receiver to her ear. "I've got a first-class passenger who needs some assistance to board and a coach customer who knows him who can help. She reached out her hand for Joey's ticket and ID. After she ran it through the machine, she said, "You can go, sir. Thank you."

Joey glanced back at Iris as he took Antonio by the arm. She motioned for him to proceed.

When Joey got him to his seat and helped him ease into it, Antonio tried to say thank you, but it came out as tank u. Joey put Antonio's bag in the overhead bin and grabbed a pillow. "You'll feel better when you wake up," he said, sliding the pillow under Antonio's head. Within a second, he was out cold. Then Joey turned and headed back to coach, Antonio's computer under his arm. He found his seat just as Iris appeared in the cabin. He felt bad as he watched her lug both bags, but there were too many people in the way for him to help. He liked how well she always seemed to handle things. He'd once heard that men often choose women like their mothers. That had made him wonder what his own mom was like. Was she strong?

When Iris was close, Joey put Antonio's computer on his seat and stood up and hoisted both bags into the overhead bin.

Iris watched him. "I do pick up a forty-pound living weight on a regular basis, you know."

That made Joey laugh. "Window or aisle?"

Iris took the window seat, picking up the computer and putting it on her lap.

"That's you-know-whose," Joey said quietly.

"I figured, since it has the *Recorder* logo on the cover." She pulled a flash drive out of her purse. "I'm going to install remote monitoring software."

Another item for his growing Iris list, thought Joey. "You're brilliant."

Iris stuck the device into the side of the computer and worked quickly. "Now we can access everything on his computer, his conversations and even videos of what he's doing," she said in a low voice. "It's time to get this back to him before he wakes up."

"No problem." Joey took the computer and headed to first class. The steward was occupied with another passenger as he slid the computer into the seat pocket and slipped back out of the cabin. When he sat back down next to Iris, he asked, "Can we take a look at his computer now?"

She shook her head. "Only when his computer is on, and we've got WIFI. We're going to have to wait until the hotel. No pistachios?"

Joey realized he hadn't felt the irritating urge for a drink that usually haunted him when he sat still for even a minute. That was definitely refreshing.

"You want some?"

"If it's not too much trouble."

He got out a bag and handed it to Iris as the plane prepared to take off.

"What are you going to do with the information we uncover in Italy?" Joey asked.

"If I can't publish it at the paper, there are other options, like the *LA Times*. Of course, I'll be kissing my career at the *Recorder* goodbye, if I do that. But this is an investigative story that needs to be told."

As she and Joey chatted, Iris thought how much she liked this. She had never experienced this kind of easy communication with a man she was interested in. It was never this companionable with Jake's father, Mark. And he had been checked out most of the time, high on pills. At first, she'd been angry to discover it was an addiction that had led to his being such a lousy father and husband. Then she decided to just let it go and vowed to never put herself in that position again.

22

When the plane touched down in Rome, it was still dark. Rubbing her eyes, Iris yawned and attempted to stretch in her seat.

"We're going to need to move quickly to keep up with Antonio when they let us out," said Joey. "I checked on him an hour ago. He was working on his computer."

"What time is it?"

"About four a.m. Italy time."

The plane's loudspeaker came to life. "*Buongiorno e benvenuti a Roma, Italia,*" said the steward. Iris listened intently. The language sounded like Spanish in some ways, but she didn't understand much of it.

"Do you speak Italian?" she asked Joey.

"A little." He was sitting up, alert, so Iris did her best to slap herself together.

As they exited the airplane onto stairs leading to the tarmac, Iris smelled diesel in the air and shivered. The wind carried a slight chill, lights twinkling in the surrounding city.

When they arrived at baggage claim, Antonio stood waiting. He looked surprisingly chipper to Iris for someone who had been nearly fall down drunk just hours before.

Staying out of sight as much as possible, they followed Antonio out of the airport, getting into a cab right behind his.

"St. Regis," said Joey, as they sat down, their bags on their laps.

The driver, who looked tired, nodded and headed away from the airport behind Antonio's taxi. They traveled for some time on a highway that eventually gave way to narrower streets and old-style architecture. As they drove, the sky began to lighten, covering the horizon with an egg-yolk orange. Gradually, the roads filled with cars with a lot of honking amongst the drivers. When the taxi began bumping over cobblestone streets, Iris admired the tall, majestic buildings on either side, many with window boxes overflowing with bright flowers. They stopped in front of an ivory-colored building featuring four impressive balustrades. Antonio got out of the taxi in front of them and headed for a Bentley parked ahead.

"Let's wait," Joey murmured to Iris, then handed the driver a credit card.

While the driver ran Joey's card, an older woman with black hair piled high on her head got out of the Bentley and embraced Antonio. Iris thought she looked to be in her sixties. The two talked, the conversation becoming more animated by the minute. Then Antonio threw up his hands and stalked toward the front doors of the hotel, the woman following.

Joey signed the credit card receipt, and he and Iris hopped out of the taxi, bags in hand. They took long strides toward the doors.

Joey wished he'd paid better attention in Italian class in high school. Antonio and the woman appeared to be arguing, but he couldn't be sure. He and Iris walked right past them without alerting Antonio's attention. They sat down on a beige couch on the other side of the lobby.

Before long, a young man sat next to them and began examining a brochure.

"Are you staying here?" asked Joey.

"Yes, I am," he said in stilted English. He sounded German. "You are American?"

"Half," said Joey. "I'm also Italian, but I don't know that much of the language. Do you?"

"Better than English," he said matter-of-factly.

"So, you know what they're talking about?" Joey gestured to Antonio and the woman, trying to sound nonchalant. "Probably a lover's quarrel or something." He grinned.

The young man glanced their way. "That is his mother, and she is not pleased with him."

"Oh, really?" said Joey. "What is she saying?"

The young man gave Joey a quizzical look.

"It helps me practice," said Joey.

He nodded and listened further. "The son is saying to the mother that he has never wanted any part of the family business. She is trying to stop him from talking in public. She wants him to check in so they can discuss the matter in private. He is saying that his life in the United States is in jeopardy."

"And I thought I had problems." Joey grinned. "Thanks."

The young man went back to his brochure.

Joey watched Antonio and his mother. She took ahold of his arms and began talking in a more soothing tone. He could see Antonio starting to cool off. Then they headed for the front desk, where the clerk checked him in quickly. A bellhop took his bags, and he and his mother looped arms and began walking toward the elevators. Suddenly, the clerk called out, "*Signor* Peroni! Your key." She rushed from behind the counter and gave it to Antonio, then returned to the desk where Joey and Iris stood.

"Do you speak English?" asked Joey.

"Of course, sir."

"My wife and I would like a room."

"Do you have reservations?"

Joey shook his head.

She checked the computer screen. "We have a small room on the fifth floor. I'm afraid that is all that is available."

"Figures that Mr. Peroni took the last big room."

The clerk did a double take. "Do you know him?"

"I know of him," said Joey. "I imagine he would have a big suite. Not like us little guys."

The woman smiled. "I haven't seen the Presidential Suite, but they say it is beautiful." She handed Joey the room keys. "Enjoy your stay. Do you need assistance with your bags?"

"I've got it," said Joey, checking the name on the woman's badge. "*Grazie*, Marcella."

"*Ciao*," she called after them as Joey took Iris's hand while they headed to the elevators.

"Good job schmoozing," Iris remarked.

"It's the one thing I'm good at." Joey pushed the up button.

When they got in an empty elevator, Iris said, "The name Peroni sounds familiar."

"It should. The Peroni family is the most powerful Italian Mafia family in this country and on this side of the world."

"Does that mean that Antonio…" Iris trailed off.

"Yes, that's exactly what that means."

23

Joey flipped on the switch, lighting up a small but pleasant suite. A gold and burgundy brocade duvet covered the bed, and matching curtains draped a floor to ceiling window across the room.

"This is nicer than I thought it would be." Joey deposited the bags at the foot of the bed. There was a coffee pot and coffee, which would come in handy right now. He was beat. Glancing over, he noticed that Iris still stood in the entryway.

"I know you're probably tired, but we can't go to sleep. It'll make the jet lag worse." He walked over and saw that she had started to cry. "Hey, what's the matter?" he said, stroking her cheek. "If you want to take a nap, that's okay."

"That's not it." Iris wiped the tears off her face, but they kept flowing.

"Let's sit down." Joey led her to an armchair and kneeled in front of her after she sat.

Iris gulped. "I'm really afraid for Jake and my mom. Maybe I should have stayed with them. I guess I'm just finally realizing how serious all of this is. I'm sorry I'm being such a big baby."

Joey got up and pulled some tissues out of a box on a nearby bureau. Kneeling again, he handed them to her. "You're not being a baby. This *is* serious. And very real. But we'll work this out. Your mom and Jake and you are going to be fine. We just need to regroup and figure out next steps."

Iris seemed to relax at his words, and some of the tension in his chest eased. "How about I make us some coffee, then we can get your computer humming and see what Antonio is up to?"

Joey took Iris's small smile as a yes.

Embarrassed by her crying jag, Iris pulled out her computer and turned it on. While Joey made coffee, she looked up the name Peroni.

"Looks like the senior Antonio Peroni died last year," Iris commented.

"I heard something about that."

Iris's web search brought up a grainy photo from six years before of the Peroni family. She leaned forward to examine it. In front sat Antonio Sr., seated in a chair, the family surrounding him. A woman who resembled the woman they'd just seen with Antonio stood next to him. Then Iris's skin went cold. "*Dios mío,*" is all she could get out.

"What?" Joey peered over her shoulder.

In the photo's background stood a man. He wasn't part of the group but standing in the back behind them. He held what appeared to be a notebook in his hands.

"That's Henry," said Iris, her voice shaky.

"Holy shit. Any idea why he's there? Could he have been writing an article?"

"It was before my time, so it's possible. But why didn't he tell me he knew Antonio before?"

"How much have you told him?"

Iris racked her brain. "I didn't tell him about my mother and Jake being in protective custody. I don't think."

"You don't think?"

Iris threw up her hands. "I don't know. We talked about Antonio, primarily."

"I'm going to text the safehouse and check up on them." Joey took out his phone and sent the message. Within thirty seconds, he got a reply and read it to Iris. "All is quiet, and everyone is fine. Let's focus on getting Antonio with his pants down, so we can get the hell out of here."

Immensely grateful to hear that her mom and Jake were okay, Iris felt like she could breathe normally again. She logged into Antonio's computer, but it appeared to be facing a wall, so she couldn't see anything.

Iris turned up the speaker, "I think he's with someone." The sound of moaning filled the room.

"Sounds like we literally caught him with his pants down." Joey laughed.

Iris was about to turn the volume down, but Joey stopped her.

"We don't want to miss anything. Kind of creepy, I know, but you'd be surprised how much good info you can get from pillow talk."

Iris sipped her coffee and waited, then started a fit of nervous giggling. God, her emotions were all over the place.

Joey grinned. "I'm glad to see a smile on your face."

"I feel like I'm losing my mind."

Just then, the computer went silent. Then Antonio said, "You can go now."

"Just like that." It was a man's voice. Iris gaped at Joey.

"If my mother comes back," came Antonio's voice, "we both know she can't catch you here."

The other man said something in Italian.

"I will tell her and the whole family about you soon," Antonio continued.

"You keep saying that, but nothing ever changes."

"This isn't easy, *il mio amore*. If my father hadn't died, we would be living our new life in the States already. I'm doing this all for us."

Neither spoke, but it sounded like someone was dressing. Then the man said, *dormi bene*, and the door opened and shut. They heard Antonio moving about, and then he spoke. "He must have called someone," Iris said.

"I'm in town, and I need the space again. No, this is the last time."

The bed covers rustled and a door shut. Then Iris heard what sounded like water. Joey started pacing in the small room.

"Does that help you think?" she said, watching him. "Because if it doesn't, can you stop? You're making me dizzy."

Joey sat down on the side of the bed. "Sorry, just trying to put all the pieces together."

"I'm saving all the files on his computer to my computer right now. We can take a good look soon at what he's been up to."

Joey nodded in approval. "Let's hope he's left a trail straight to his noose."

After she had saved all of Antonio's files, Iris began opening the first of his Excel spreadsheets and tried to make sense of the numbers.

"Can I take a look?" asked Joey. Iris passed him the computer.

After a couple of minutes, Joey whistled. "Pretty sure these are Antonio's records of sales, including names of buyers and how much they've spent. This could be explosive on many levels."

Joey quieted when there was a knock on Antonio's door and the sound of it opening.

"What the hell are you doing here?" Antonio cried.

"I came to make sure you don't screw this whole thing up."

Iris gasped and said, "That's Henry."

24

Antonio's door slammed. "Nothing is going to get screwed up, except for someone tracking you here. What the hell were you thinking?"

"I'm thinking I gave up my career as a journalist—a prize winning one, by the way—to bet on whatever you want to call this. Where are we at?"

"If you're referring to the next shipment, I've arranged for the transfer already. Once it's done, then I'm out."

"As long as I get my cut and the exclusive for my book, I'm fine. I don't care what you do."

"You and that damn book. I'll be glad when you finish that thing and are out of my life."

"The feeling is mutual. Meanwhile, I think one of the paper's writers is here on your trail."

Iris heard a thud, as if someone had slammed a glass down. "Brown hair and green eyes? I knew I recognized her. She was with someone."

"He's undercover narcotics with the Santa Ana PD," said Henry.

"Why am I just now hearing about this?"

"I got a flight out as soon as I could. Just calm down."

"Calm down. An undercover narc is here."

"He has no jurisdiction, and I'm taking care of him, anyway. Not sure what to do about her, though."

"What do you mean?"

"She's my protégé."

Iris's skin felt cold.

"There is no room for sentimentality here."

"No? What about your lover?"

Iris heard what sounded like a scuffle, then someone gasping. "Don't you ever mention him again," Antonio warned. The gasping gave way to labored breathing as Antonio continued. "I'll put some of my men on her, if you can't take care of it."

"No need to get violent. Do what you want with her." Henry cleared his throat a couple of times. "So where did you see them?"

"They were in the airport and on the plane." Antonio began cussing in Italian, then their connection went dead.

"Looks like Antonio figured out we bugged his laptop," said Joey, moving to close their bags.

Iris sat there, stunned at Henry's involvement.

"We gotta go," said Joey. "Henry plans to take care of us, and Antonio probably remembers we're staying here."

Iris quickly shut down her laptop and slid it into its case. Joey had already grabbed their bags and was in the hallway, heading for the elevator. When it arrived, Iris entered first, then turned around to hold the door open for Joey. She gasped to see that two men had him at gunpoint.

"Go!" he yelled, as she banged on the door close button. One of the men stuck his leg into the elevator. Iris stomped on his shin, and he pulled it back, howling. She pushed the button again, and the door slid shut before he could stop it from closing.

Trying to catch her breath as the elevator descended toward the lobby, Iris willed herself to remain as calm as possible. She rushed out the open doors, then spied a women's restroom. Racing over, she ran inside and into a stall. Closing and latching the door, she struggled to figure out what to do, but the thudding in her head made it hard to think. Think, Iris, she urged herself. Her cellphone was in the bag Joey was carrying, but she had her laptop. Hands shaking, she opened her computer and logged into the hotel's free WIFI. Then she pulled up a VOIP line and called Aunt Joanna's cellphone.

"Iris?"

"*Tia*! I need your help. I'm in Italy. At the St. Regis, hiding in the women's bathroom in the lobby."

"Okay, slow down. What are you doing there?"

"It's a long story, but they have Joey, and I think they're going to kill him."

"Joey who?"

"Landau. He's undercover narcotics."

There was silence on the other end of the line.

"*Tia*?"

"What in the hell are you doing with Landau in Italy?"

"Aunt Joanna, I know something happened between you two. I'm working on a story here. Please, can you help?"

"Of course, but I'm in Amsterdam right now. I can have someone there to get you within twenty minutes. And I can get a helicopter to Rome. I should be there in about three hours."

"What about Joey?"

"We'll talk about Joey when I get there. You stay put. The code word when they come will be Delia."

When Iris heard the door to the bathroom open five minutes later, she quietly raised her legs so they weren't visible. Holding her breath, she waited while someone walked into the room. Then the person's phone buzzed. "We can't find her." It was a man. He sounded American. "Stationary store near the Trevi. We'll be there in ten minutes."

Just then the door to the bathroom opened, and a woman screeched.

"Sorry, wrong bathroom," said the man as the woman muttered something in Italian.

Iris waited a couple of minutes while the woman entered a stall, went to the bathroom and left. She knew she should wait for the agent coming to get her, but her aunt had probably told the person to take her to a safehouse, where she wouldn't be able to help Joey. Peeking out of the bathroom's main door, she saw no signs of anyone looking for her in the lobby. She slipped out and walked quickly to the front door, grabbing a map of Rome from a display case on the way out. Checking the map outside of the hotel, she was glad to see that the Trevi was only four blocks away.

Joey was relieved when the guy who had stormed back into the hotel to find Iris returned emptyhanded. His face an angry mask of stone, he got into the car's passenger seat and slammed the door. "The store," he ordered the driver. Without checking oncoming traffic, the man started driving.

"I guess my reputation precedes me," Joey remarked, the twist tie binding his wrists biting into his skin.

"Shut up, or we'll gag you, too," said the man in the front seat.

"Where we going?"

"You want me to gag him, Jenkins?" asked the guy sitting next to Joey, his gun trained on him.

The man in the front ignored them both as they made their way through the streets of Rome. Joey wondered where Iris had gone.

"Landau, I'm Agent Molinaro. You were hit. Lie back down."

Joey struggled to sit up, but there was something wrong with his shoulder. "I need to stop them from killing Dawn."

"She sustained several GSWs, but she's still alive. For now."

Joey heard the ambulance in the distance. The smell of blood filled his nostrils.

"Oh, my God, this is all my fault."

"Are you under the influence of alcohol, Detective Landau?"

Joey shook his head, denying the obvious. Then he closed his eyes. Maybe he should just give in and leave. Let them concentrate on saving Dawn. This was all his fault, anyway. Every bit of it.

Sounding like she was talking to him from a distance, Joey heard Agent Molinaro urge him. "Stay with me, Landau. Help is on the way."

25

Iris rushed into the only stationary store she spotted near the Trevi Fountain. Inside, an Italian woman greeted her.

"*Buongiorno*, may I help you find something?" The woman wore a red smock over a yellow dress and had a matching faux red flower tucked into her hair. She stood arranging a shelf containing ribbons and bows.

Glancing around at the display cases overflowing with multi-colored stationary items, Iris replied, "You have quite a selection here. I'm going to look around and will let you know if I have any questions."

"Very well, we have a special on dye cutouts today. Fifty percent off. And if you buy a pen, you get one free." The woman went back to organizing.

Iris walked toward a display of cards and began pulling them out and pretending to read them.

"Are you seeking a card for anyone in particular?" the woman asked.

"For my mother," said Iris.

The woman walked over to the card display where Iris stood. "Is your mother the serious sort, or does she enjoy a bit of levity?"

"I'd say she would enjoy a humorous card, although she's serious when she's cross with me."

The woman laughed. "I would suggest looking at the cards on the blue rack. I think you'll find something your mother would like there."

The front door opened, and the woman glanced back towards it, tension suddenly covering her face. "Excuse me a moment." She turned and headed to the front of the store.

Unsure who had entered, Iris kept her back to the door.

"The boss needs the back room." It was the voice of the man in the bathroom! Iris snuck a quick peek, then returned to acting as if she was shopping.

The two continued their conversation in hushed tones. As Iris pulled out cards without seeing them, her heart hammered in her chest. All she wanted to do was scream at the man and ask what they did with Joey.

The front door opened and closed, and then the woman's heels tapped on the wood floor as she headed towards the back. Keys jingled and a door opened and shut. Iris wasn't sure what to do next. Had the man recognized her? Should she leave? But they might be putting Joey in the back room at this very moment. One thing she did know, she had to hide her computer. Pulling on the card display rack, she found that it moved. Carefully, she slid it forward, then went around to the back and discovered a ledge on the backside of the shelf. Setting her computer into the shelf, she carefully scooted the rack back into place up against the wall. Just as she finished, the door to the back room swung open and the woman returned.

"Forgive my rudeness," she said. "Have you chosen a card for your mother?"

"I remembered some other relatives to buy for, so I'm still looking," Iris replied, then heard what sounded like a thud coming from the back room.

When they arrived at their destination, a building next to the Trevi

Fountain, the driver drove into an alley and stopped the car. Jenkins checked a back door that appeared to be locked and went around to the front of the building.

"I've got backup coming," said Joey. "I'd bail if I were you."

The guy with the gun grabbed Joey by the arm and jerked him out of the car. When the door of the building opened, he pushed Joey inside.

"Sit down," ordered Jenkins, pointing to a chair in the center of a small room filled with stacked boxes. A worktable ran the length of one wall.

"Who you waiting for? Antonio?"

Jenkins glared at Joey.

"They tell you Antonio is bailing after the next shipment? And that Henry is going to get a big cut and run, too?"

That caused Jenkins to hesitate for a fraction of a second. "The gag is still an option, Landau. Shut up."

Joey continued. "It's a matter of time before Antonio gets rid of you and your men. He's not going to leave loose ends when he flies off with his boyfriend."

"Gag him," said Jenkins.

The man pulled a handkerchief out of his back pocket and stuffed it into Joey's mouth. Jenkins looked like he was starting to get cagey. "I'm going to make a call," he said. "Keep an eye on him."

He went out into what looked like a stationary store and shut the door. This was Joey's chance. Jumping up and jerking his head to one side, he spit out the gag and gave the guy a hard jab to the nose with both bound hands, knocking him out and to the floor. He ran to the worktable and lifted the lever to a paper cutter. As carefully as possible, he sawed through the twist tie, freeing his hands. Joey grabbed the guy's gun and headed for the door to the alley. Opening it carefully, he saw the driver standing a foot away smoking a cigarette. He took him by surprise with the butt of the gun, knocking him sideways and onto the pavement. Then he raced down the alley, putting the gun into the back of his pants and pulling his shirt over it. Rounding the corner, Joey blended into the crowd.

Joey opened his eyes and tried to focus. It looked like Royce's face swimming in front of him. Then he heard a beeping sound and saw a bag and tubing. He felt something in his arm. He must be in the hospital.

"Stay calm," said Royce.

Joey struggled to form the words. "Where's Pop?"

Royce's eyes registered something Joey didn't understand, then he said, "You've been shot, you need to rest. Close your eyes."

"I gotta talk to Pop. Tell him I'm sorry I took his truck."

Royce nodded. "You just rest, boy. Give yourself a fighting chance."

26

Iris struggled to decide what to do. If she could just get back there, she might find Joey. But how? Just then, the door to the back room swung open. The man walked out and pulled out his cellphone.

Iris froze. She was right in his line of sight, and it was a matter of moments before he saw her. Sure enough, he glanced her way and yelled, "You!"

Iris turned to run, but he was behind her within seconds, grabbing her by the hair to prevent her from moving forward. She opened her mouth to yell, when he clamped his large hand over and jerked her head backwards.

"One sound out of you, and I'll break your pretty neck right here," he warned her as he pulled her toward the back. When he pushed her into the back room, he announced, "Look what I found." Then he yelled, "Damn it all." A man lay in the middle of the floor unmoving. Holding her by one arm, he went to the door that opened onto the back alley and peered out. Another man lay in the alleyway. When the man in the room began to moan and sat up, he shouted at him, "What the hell happened?"

"He broke my nose!"

"Where'd he go?"

"I don't know. You left, and next thing I know he's punching me in the face."

The driver stumbled into the room.

"You two are blithering idiots. The boss will be here any minute. I should shoot you both before he gets here."

As if on cue, a car pulled up in the alleyway. The man was still holding Iris's arm in a vice grip when Antonio and Henry walked in. Henry looked surprised to see her.

"I thought you said you caught him and couldn't find her?" Antonio demanded.

"How could you, Henry?" Iris cried out. "All for a book?"

Her mentor approached and said simply, "Yes, Iris, you should understand that more than anyone. The story comes first."

"You taught me to seek the truth. Not mow down anyone who gets in my way."

Henry shook his head. "How do you think people get to the top in any field? You were always a bit naïve, Iris."

"Enough with the family reunion." Antonio interrupted. "We need to get Landau back here."

"Where would he go, Iris?" Henry asked. "Tell us, and we can spare your mother and son."

Iris stared at Henry dumbfounded. She couldn't believe that she had worshipped this man. He had seemed so kind and genuine. "Jake and my mother, Henry? You couldn't."

"He might not be able to, but I can," said Antonio. "Now tell us where you think he went."

Iris's mind whirred. Were they bluffing? God, how she wished she'd waited for her aunt.

"I'm losing my patience," said Antonio, who waved his phone in the air. "It's time my people make a visit to the safehouse."

"Don't! I'll tell you where Joey said to meet in case we were separated."

The only place Iris could possibly be was the hotel. Joey prayed she had gone back to the room.

When he got there, he went to the front desk and asked for another room key, saying he'd left his in the room. The clerk on duty gave him a funny look. "Your wife also locked her key in the room."

"When?" Joey asked hopefully.

"Just a few minutes ago."

Relief washed through Joey as he hurried to the room. This whole case had gone to shit, but he could handle that. As long as Iris was okay. He vowed to put her on a plane home immediately. When he put the key in the lock and opened the door, he came face-to-face with Joanna Molinaro. She drew her gun and kept it on him.

"Where is Iris?" she demanded.

"She's not here?"

"No, Landau, she's not. She called me three hours ago from the bathroom downstairs. She was supposed to wait until help came. I had an agent in the area, but when she got to the bathroom, no one was there."

"There has to be an explanation," said Joey.

He watched Joanna's brown eyes darken. She said in a low, even tone, her gun steady, "If something happened to my niece because of you, I will kill you, Landau."

"If something happened to her, I'll take the bullet. Can you remove that from my face now? We're wasting time."

Joanna lowered her gun. She looked at Joey's wrists. "What happened to you?"

"I was abducted from the hotel, right before you must have talked to Iris. They took me to a back room of a stationary store near the Trevi, but I got away."

"Is there any way Iris could have known where they took you?"

"I don't see how. We were monitoring Antonio Peroni for smuggling black tar heroin into Santa Ana, but he figured out that we bugged his laptop. We didn't have the location at that point."

"We? How long have you been doing whatever it is you're doing with my niece?" Joanna eyed the bed, which they hadn't slept in, and looked back at Joey.

"Can we reserve this conversation for later?"

"Fine, but we've got a lot to talk about when this is all done." Joanna's stance softened and she holstered her gun.

While she called contacts at the Rome police department, Joey paced. When she hung up, she said, "They're checking the traffic cameras. In the meantime, tell me everything that has happened since you met each other, and don't leave anything out."

Joey started from the top. All the while praying that Iris would come walking through the door any minute.

27

After Joey finished telling Joanna everything about the case, he took a deep breath and added, "Look, I know you have no reason to trust me. I wouldn't trust me. I screwed up big time that night. It ruined a good agent's career, and she almost died. I live with that every day. But I've been clean for more than a year now, and I've worked hard for my sobriety. I know none of that excuses my behavior. But I can tell you for a fact that I care about Iris, and I'll do anything to get her back safely, including taking a bullet for her."

Joanna eyed Joey for a moment. "Let's hope it doesn't come to that, but it's good to know. My niece is headstrong. I'm sure she would have come to Italy with or without you—" Joanna's phone rang, cutting her off midsentence. She listened, then jotted an address on hotel stationary before hanging up.

"Traffic cameras caught Iris walking on foot toward the Trevi. She must have found out about the store. I've got an associate in the Rome police sending a car to pick us up and take us there. I also called Interpol. There's a bunch of agencies that want to catch the Peronis with their hands in the cookie jar, but it must be airtight. Frankly, I don't really care, as long as we get my niece back."

· · ·

When they pulled up at the store, Joey and Joanna headed toward the back of the building, while two officers went in through the front. The alley was empty. Joey tried the back door; it was unlocked. Nodding to Joanna, who moved to one side of the door, he pushed the door open, staying to the side. Silence from within. Joey jumped in front of the door, gun drawn, and his heart fell. In the center of the empty room was a pool of blood.

"No, no, no, no, no," Joey said as he approached the blood, which looked fresh. Joanna was right behind him.

"We don't know that it's Iris's blood."

Joey squared his shoulders and shook his head to clear it. She was right. He glanced around the small room. There didn't appear to be any cameras back here.

Just then one of the Italian police officers entered the room. He glanced at the blood. "We have signs of a struggle in the front of the store."

"Can we get a CSI team here to test the blood?" Joanna asked. The officer nodded. She said to Joey, "I'm going to check out the store. See what else you can find here."

When she left, Joey heard what sounded like a moan from the other side of the room.

"Hello?"

Another moan, then a big box leaning against the wall moved slightly. He pulled it back and revealed a bound and gagged woman in a yellow dress. Pushing the box to the side, he pulled the handkerchief from her mouth. Gratitude filled her eyes, then apprehension.

"It's okay, I'm here to help you. Are you the store manager?"

She nodded.

"Do you speak English? Was someone shot?"

"A man," she sputtered.

"Was there a woman with them?"

"Yes, they took her."

"Did you hear them say where they were going?" Joey helped the woman to her feet as Joanna returned.

"The Peronis own this store. The son, Antonio, was here," she said. "I think he mentioned their house near Lake Bracciano."

"That lake is northwest of here," said Joanna. "My sources say Antonio has been sighted heading south. I wouldn't be surprised if they're going to Sicily."

"I think we should cover both directions," Joey said. "I'm fine with checking the lake house. I just need a vehicle."

Joanna made a phone call. "The Peronis do have a house by the lake. I'll text you the address. You good to go there on your own? I need to put what manpower I've been able to cajole from local law enforcement towards the most credible lead." She handed him keys and a cellphone. "Take the rental car I've been driving. I'll go in the squad car. My number is programmed into the phone. Keep me posted."

Joey headed out just as a paramedic arrived. As he climbed behind the wheel of the rental, he was glad to see the vehicle had GPS. He punched in the address. It was a good forty minutes away.

Thankful that Iris was still alive, his stomach clenched in worry when he thought about what Antonio and his crew had planned for her. Most likely, they wanted to know how much she knows about the operation, and what she'd written, and who'd seen it. Where was her computer? he wondered.

They had removed the bullet and stitched Joey back up and told him to rest, but he yanked on his IVs. He had to see Dawn, to know she was going to be okay.

"What the hell are you doing?" Joanna sprang up from where she sat by his hospital bed. She motioned to take hold of his arm, but he jerked it away.

"I'm okay. This hardly hurts. Where's Dawn? I need to say I'm sorry."

"You can't see her. She's in surgery. Has been for the past two hours. The best thing you can do is rest."

"Surgery? Why that long?"

"It's bad, Landau. The bullet shattered and hit nerves in her spinal column."

Joey felt the energy drain from his body. When the nurse came into his room a few minutes later and asked him if he was in pain, he lied and asked for morphine.

28

As Joey traveled the highway away from Rome toward the Peroni lake house, his impatience eased up. The traffic snarl in Rome and incessant honking had set his already frazzled nerves afire. He glanced out the window as the land of the Mediterranean slipped by. Eventually, the road opened, and wheat-colored pastureland dotted by small farmhouses unfolded next to the highway.

When the GPS indicated that he was about fifteen minutes from his destination, Joey began driving amongst pine forests. A house in an out-of-the-way location like this offered a great opportunity to have hush-hush meetings with heavy hitters. The place was probably a fortress.

As the road narrowed in a dense area of trees, he slowed and calculated his next move. Driving up and asking for entrance into the villa seemed like a farfetched idea. Joey recalled one op in the Santa Monica Mountains where the owner of the estate had set up an electronic surveillance system around the perimeter that shocked anyone who tried to cross it. Not having intel on this place had Joey at a complete disadvantage. He decided to try driving up to the house.

Lined with olive trees, the driveway stopped in front of a large metal gate. He watched as a camera on the side of the gate moved around. Then, to his amazement, the gate began opening. Joey quickly drove the car through. The drive snaked up to a villa sitting on a hill. Citrus trees dotted the lawn, where a giant three-tiered fountain bubbled and splashed in the late afternoon sun.

Joey stopped and pulled to the side of the drive. He picked up his gun from the passenger side and hid it under his jacket. At the door, he lifted the brass knocker and rapped several times.

A woman came to the door, flashing Joey a broad smile. "*Ciao*, can I help you, *signor*?" He was about to open his mouth when a woman's voice called from inside, "Who is it, Stella?"

"My name is Joey. I'm looking for Antonio."

The maid pulled the door open wide, revealing the woman Joey had seen outside of the hotel. "May I ask your surname?" The woman eyed him carefully.

"Joey Cooper, *signora*."

The woman came closer until she stood just a few feet away from Joey. "Forgive my rudeness," she said. "I am *Signora* Peroni, Antonio's mother. Please come in and wait for him."

Joey walked across the threshold, senses on overdrive. He took in the foyer with its teak side table on which lay a pile of mail, and above that pegs for hats. There was an umbrella stand and a rack for shoes.

"Come into the living room." Signora Peroni turned and Joey followed. She was dressed in a blue pants suit. Gold bracelets jangled on her wrists. The walls in the living room were decorated with paintings boasting bright splashes of color. The floor shined to a polished gleam, and a grand piano took centerstage in the room.

"If I may ask," said Joey as he sat down in an armchair. "When was the last time you saw Antonio?"

The woman settled onto a plush maroon sofa. "A day or so ago. Now what is your business with my son?"

"It is mutual business and somewhat urgent. Do you have any idea where he may be?"

"I'm afraid I don't keep tabs on him, but I expect him back soon."

The maid walked up with a tray containing a bottle of water and two glasses.

"You can leave the tray here Stella." The woman poured Joey and herself tall glasses of water, then handed him one. "Fresh from our well," she said, raising her glass and taking a sip.

"*Grazie*," said Joey. He took a swallow, then set the glass down. "How long have you had this place?" he asked.

"It has been in the family for decades," she replied. Joey heard her saying something else about how the place was passed down from generation to generation, but he suddenly felt woozy, like his head was too heavy for his body.

When Joey awoke, he was bound and lying on the floor somewhere. He opened his eyes to see Iris also tied up and lying a few feet away, her face to his.

"I should have known better than to accept a drink of anything," he grumbled. "I came to get you."

Iris smiled. "My hero."

Joey started to laugh, but he had a hell of a headache. "I met up with your Aunt Joanna. She went chasing a different lead. I took the short straw and came here." Joey glanced around from his vantage point and realized they were in a wine cellar. Footsteps descended the stairs, and Antonio walked into the room.

"I see you came to find your friend. I have my own friends at the *forze di polizia* in Rome. They are giving Agent Molinaro, what do you Americans say, a run for her money."

"What happened to Henry?" Iris asked.

"Let's not talk about that. What do you know about my business interests?"

"Just that you're a publisher that's been around Orange County for the past forty years," said Joey. "Can you let us go now so we can get back to saving the world."

Antonio sighed. "I see this is going to take some time. Jenkins," he called out. "Bring down our persuasion tool."

Jenkins came into the wine cellar with a cattle prod. Joey saw Iris's eyes widen in fear.

"Are either of you familiar with the cattle prod? This is one of my favorite tools for loosening up tongues. The Chinese have been known to use the device quite successfully for torture."

"Who first?" Jenkins asked Antonio.

"Let me think about this for a moment." Antonio pulled a bottle of wine out of the wall and examined the label, then slid it back in.

"I vote for him," he said, pointing to Joey.

Jenkins approached Joey, and Iris cried out, "We'll tell you whatever you want to know."

"Henry did say you were pretty bright," Antonio mused.

"We have all of the files on your computer," Joey said calmly. "If anything happens to us, they will be immediately sent to the Italian and U.S. authorities and Interpol."

"You expect me to believe that?"

"Including the Excel sheets containing who buys the heroin," added Iris.

Joey watched unease fill Antonio's eyes. "Where's the computer? Answer me, or else this cattle prod is going to be leaving some scars."

29

"I can tell you where it is, but the computer won't unlock without my fingerprint," said Iris.

"That's easily solved," said Jenkins to Antonio. "I'll just go get the computer and destroy it."

"It's not that simple. I have the records stored in a cloud account, too."

"You want me to go get it and bring it back?" Jenkins asked Antonio.

"We don't have time for that. I need to be at that meeting tonight, and my mother wants these two out of here."

Two of Antonio's men threw Joey and Iris into the back of a panel van, but not before binding their hands and legs. Joey heard Iris yelp as they slammed the door shut and locked it. "You okay?" he asked. They both lay on their sides facing one another. Joey struggled to push himself closer to her.

"He was pretty rough when he shoved me into the truck," said Iris.

Joey eyed her. "I'm really sorry about all of this."

"Hey, I could have stayed home with my mom and Jake. I knew what I might be getting into."

"Speaking of knowing what you're getting into. There's something I need to tell you. I know this isn't the best time, but I—"

The front doors of the van opened then, and it sounded like two men got in. The engine fired to life, and the vehicle started moving.

"You what?" asked Iris.

Joey sighed and looked into her eyes. God, how he wanted to come clean and tell Iris everything. About her aunt, about his past.

"About what happened with my aunt?"

"That and more," said Joey.

"You don't have to if you don't want to. Later."

Joey didn't want to state the obvious, but they had no guarantees there would be a later. "No, I have to tell you now. If that's okay?"

Iris smiled as the van bumped into a pothole and up and out. "I'm a little tied up at the moment, but it's okay."

That's what Joey loved about Iris. She could take a bad situation and always make it better.

He took a deep breath and hoped that same look he saw in her eyes now didn't change once he told her the truth.

"I'm an alcoholic. In recovery for more than a year now. There was a time when I was drunk pretty much 24/7." Joey stopped and waited.

"Go on," she said, her eyes softening.

"I could tell you it's because I grew up without a mother, and there were some occasions at AA meetings that I whined about that, but the fact is that me and alcohol just don't work. I don't have an off switch."

"Like Mark with pills," Iris said quietly.

This was exactly what Joey feared. The comparison and then the conclusions. "Yeah, I guess you could say so."

"But you managed to quit," Iris added.

"Not before nearly killing someone else and myself. That's where your aunt came in. We had a sting operation going. Me and another agent, Dawn Paige, were posing as a couple who sold drugs. Cocaine. We'd been working the case for months. We infiltrated a Ukrainian ring doing the smuggling. The guy in charge was ready to hand us the proverbial key to the castle. Give us all the business in Southern California so he could go deal with things back home. We had him on tape and everything. Trouble was, my drinking sometimes got out of hand when I was undercover. We did a lot of business in underground clubs, and the vodka was flowing, and I wasn't saying no. Dawn kept warning me, but I told her I was fine, that it was all an act." Joey stopped and took a breath.

"But you weren't fine."

"No, far from it. I'm not making excuses here, but you have no idea how hard it is not to drink if that's your weakness. I thought I was just dosing, you know. Drinking just enough to clear my head, but it was having the opposite effect. One night, the Ukrainian leader was supposed to put me and Dawn in charge, then the feds, led by your aunt, were going to sweep in and clean up. But I was at my pop's drinking, and I lost track of time. When I got a text from Dawn asking where I was, I freaked. She was all alone at the meet. My pop tried to stop me from going, but I stole his truck. I'm not sure exactly what happened once I got there, because I blacked out. When I came to, I was on the ground with a bullet in my shoulder, and your aunt was leaning over me."

"What happened to Dawn?"

Joey swallowed the lump that always formed when he thought back to that night. "It turns out the meet that night was actually to get rid of us, not to put us in charge. Because of me. I had gotten drunk the night before and said something that tipped off the Ukrainians. Dawn got shot in the back. The bullet shattered bones in her spinal column. She survived, but she can't walk. I went to see her once I became sober. She was the first person on my apology list when I was working the steps. I was shocked she forgave me. Her father had a problem with drinking. I guess she kind of understood the battle."

"That's good," said Iris.

"There was a casualty that night, though. My pop. When he heard I'd been shot, he had a heart attack. For a long time, I blamed myself. But the doctors told me it was bound to happen. It was just a matter of when. If I'd been there, though, I might have saved him. Instead, I was drunk at a crime scene."

"Oh, Joey." Iris's eyes clouded with compassion. "I'm so sorry."

Just then, the van stopped. The sound of traffic and honking surrounded the vehicle. Joey heard yelling in Italian.

"We're probably close to the store. We better come up with a plan."

"I have an idea," said Iris.

When the van stopped, the goon who opened the back door looked down at Iris, shocked. "What's wrong with her?"

"I don't know. She passed out a while ago."

The man called to Antonio, who came and looked in. "What's her problem?"

"I've been calling to her trying to get her to respond, but she's passed out," Joey said.

"We need her to tell us where the computer is and that blasted cloud storage." Antonio began slapping her across the face, but Iris didn't flinch. "Untie her feet," he said to his henchman. "See if she can stand."

Joey watched in amazement as the man did as instructed, but Iris crumpled to the ground, lifeless.

"Let's get them out of the alley before we attract attention. Where's Luigi?" asked Antonio.

"Searching the store for the computer. Nothing yet."

"Get her into the back room, then drag him in there with her," Antonio instructed. "I'm going to check on the progress."

The man carried Iris in and soon came back for Joey. When the guy went to pick him up, Joey was glad he'd kept up on his boxing training. He was able to become dead weight in the man's grasp. As the guy struggled, Joey remarked, "Untie my legs, and I can walk."

The guy ignored Joey and kept trying to pick him up with enough difficulty that he stopped for a moment. Then came what Joey had been praying for. Iris clocked the guy on the back of the head with the paper cutter. He fell into the alley, and Iris hurried to untie Joey's hands and feet.

Once untied, Joey used the ties to bind the guy on the ground. He lifted him into the van and slammed the door shut.

"Go and call your aunt. I've got to see this through with Antonio."

Iris frowned and nodded, turning and heading down the alley.

In the backroom, Joey dug around in drawers until he found scissors. He slid them into his back pocket, then positioned himself by the door to the store and waited. He didn't have to wait long. Luigi opened the door and walked into the room, swinging around just as Joey smashed him in the face with the paper cutter. He fell back, crying out. Antonio came rushing in with a gun pointed at Joey's head.

"Game's over, Landau. Tell me where that computer is, or I'll shoot your face off." Just then Iris appeared behind Antonio shoving him toward Joey, who had pulled the scissors out. When Antonio made contact, the scissors slid into his chest, and the gun went off, a bullet ricocheting off the ceiling. Antonio's eyes registered shock as he fell back on the floor, his body soon becoming limp.

"I told you to go get your aunt!" Joey cried. "Do you ever listen?"

"Never has listened," said Joanna from behind her. "Nice push, by the way."

Iris swung around. "*Tia!*"

"I hoped you two might be here after the local PD got a disturbance call. I see we have eliminated the threat. Too bad he took all the evidence with him. We found his computer in his hotel room and are checking computers at the *Recorder*, but it looks like everything was wiped clean. We're pretty sure his mother is the mastermind, but we have no way of proving that."

Iris smiled and motioned for Joanna and Joey to follow her into the store. They watched as she moved a card display case away from the wall and reached in the back to pull out her laptop. She handed it to Joanna. "There's an encrypted file in there that contains everything that was on his computer."

"I could kiss you right now, Iris, but I think I'll leave that up to him." Joanna gestured to Joey with her head. "I want to get this to the PD's computer lab immediately. The chief will be happy to hear that he just might get the Peronis, after all."

"I thought the computer needed your fingerprint to unlock it?" asked Joey.

"Calculated lie." Iris grinned.

"That's my niece," Joanna said proudly.

When Joanna went to talk to some police officers, Joey turned to Iris, waiting, hoping that she'd rush into his arms. But she didn't. Iris looked at the floor and back up again at Joey, and his heart plummeted.

30

When Iris still didn't say anything, Joey decided to make it easier on her.

"I understand. I get it. I'd run away from me, too."

Iris came toward him then. She took his face in her hands. "That's not what I'm thinking at all."

"You're not?" Hope seeped into his chest.

She shook her head. "Answer something for me honestly. No denying."

Joey nodded. "I'll tell you anything."

"When you said you almost died, you weren't referring to the gunshot wound, were you?"

Joey wanted to look down at the floor, but he willed himself to keep his eyes directed at Iris's open and honest ones. "No, after Pop died, I was in a really bad way. I stayed at his house and just kept drinking. One night, I…" Joey trailed off. "I … almost blew my brains out." There. He'd said it out loud.

"But you didn't."

"Royce, my boxing trainer, happened to knock on my door. He talked me off the ledge. He urged me to go to AA. I've been clean since."

Iris kissed Joey lightly on the mouth. Relief and joy rushing through him, he returned the kiss, sweetly, gently, gratefully.

When they pulled apart, Iris said, "I have an idea, if you're open to it."

"I love ideas."

"What do you think about us staying in Rome for another couple days and doing some sightseeing, since we're here? I'd say let's stay a week, but I want to get home to my mom and Jake."

Joey smiled in response.

"I'll take that as a yes."

They found Joanna sorting out the details with the local PD.

"You're probably looking for your bags," she said, pointing to them sitting on the side table. "They were found in one of Antonio's vehicles. You can take them."

She addressed Joey. "We have everything we need. I'm going to put a call in to your boss at the Santa Ana PD and brief him on what happened. Iris, they've returned Jake and your mom home safe and sound."

"Thanks so much, *Tia*. Is it okay if we go?"

"In a minute. I want to talk to Joey first."

"I'll go call my mom and Jake while you do that."

Joey squared his shoulders and went to stand in front of Joanna.

She sighed. "It's obvious that Iris really cares about you, and it appears that you've cleaned up your act. Just be careful with Iris. She's tough, but she has a marshmallow heart."

Joey swallowed the lump starting to form in his throat. "That's what I admire about her, among many other things. And thank you."

"Don't thank me now," said Joanna matter-of-factly. "Like I told you before, you break my niece's heart, I'll shoot you."

"You said you'd shoot me if she got hurt. The rules are changing, I see."

"Rules always change, Landau. Now get out of here before I change my mind."

When Joey found Iris, she was smiling into her phone. "I love you, too, munchkin, and I'll be home in just three days, okay. You listen to your *abuelita*." Joey watched as she gave him loud kisses and then ended the call.

"All set?" he asked.

"Yes, Jake was so happy to be back to normal that it hardly registered that I won't be home for a few more days."

"Since we're staying, there's something I'd like to do." Joey put his bag on the ground and unzipped it, rummaging around and then pulling out an envelope.

"Is that what I think it is?" Iris asked.

"Yeah, the letter Pop gave me years ago about my mom."

Iris took the envelope from his grasp and turned it over. "You didn't open it. I doubt I'd have that much restraint."

"If I didn't open it, I didn't have to face the possibility that my mom just didn't want me," said Joey quietly.

"But you don't know that was the reason. You going to open it now?"

Joey nodded. "How about we sit at the fountain?" They walked to the Trevi and managed to find a spot on the edge of the large pool of water that sat in front of the fountain. Tourists stood throwing money into the water and taking photos of themselves. Joey took a deep breath and opened the envelope, pulling out several pages written in Pop's scrawl. The noises surrounding him vanished as he read the letter, hearing his father's voice as he did so.

Son, I know I never told you much about your mom. She and I met during a different time. I was stationed in Italy, and what can I say. We were young, and we were foolish. When she ended up pregnant with you, I did what I thought was the right thing and asked her to marry me. She wanted to stay in Italy, but I talked her into moving to the States. To say she didn't belong here was an understatement. She couldn't seem to adjust, and she was miserable. She tried to do her art and that didn't work. In the end, I realized it was best for her to go home to Italy and to her art. I know this is hard to understand, but the truth is that your mom was thinking of you and your best interest. It would have killed me to see you go to Italy, and I wasn't going to be able to get work there to support us. Could we have worked all of this out if we really tried? Maybe, but what's done is done, son. Now that you're eighteen, I want you to get ahold of her if you choose to. Her name is Catarina Berone. I don't have an address for her, but I know they have her paintings on display at the Bella Gallery in Rome. And most likely others. Maybe they can direct you to her. I love you son, and I hope you believe me that your mom does, too. She asked me to send her photos of you throughout the years to the gallery, and I've done that.

Joey handed the letter to Iris.

After she read it, she gave it back to him. "Do you want to try and locate her? I think I saw that gallery on the way from the hotel."

"Yes, let's do it. Right now."

They made their way back toward the hotel, and after a couple of blocks found the gallery, tucked away on a side street.

"Looks like they're open," said Joey. "You first." He pulled the door open and motioned for Iris to enter.

A hush surrounded them as they walked into the gallery. They were greeted by a wall covered in large canvases featuring splashes of rainbow colors. The Italian woman at the front desk glanced up as they entered. "*Ciao*. May I help you?" she asked in perfect English. She wore a jet blue silk pantsuit and diamond pendant earrings.

"We're looking for someone. An artist you represent," said Joey. "Catarina Berone."

The woman's smile turned to a frown. "We did represent Catarina, but she passed away last year after a long battle with cancer. Did you know her?" She came from around the desk and walked up to Joey, something flickering in her eyes when she looked at his face.

"I...no, but I was hoping to meet her." Joey felt disappointment and regret overtake him. He turned to leave.

"Would you like to see our collection of her work? I think you would find it quite remarkable," the woman asked.

"That would be very nice," said Iris when Joey didn't answer.

She led them toward the back of the gallery and pointed to a long wall filled with portraits. "I'll let you take a good look at them. I'm here to answer any questions you may have." She walked back to the front desk.

Iris's heart hitched as she watched Joey's face. She could feel his sadness at finding out his mother had died. But as his eyes scanned the many portraits on the wall, she saw his expression change, become more hopeful and peaceful. Iris turned her attention to the paintings, soon realizing that the wall contained portrait after portrait of Joey as he grew up. It started with a painting of an infant bundled in a blue blanket, then a toddler in a small, plastic pool. He gazed up at whoever was watching him with a mischievous grin on his face.

"I remember that plastic pool," said Joey. He continued down the wall, studying each painting in the progression of his life through his mother's eyes. At times stopping and staring for minutes.

"That's a nice portrait of you on your graduation day," Iris commented when they arrived near the end of the paintings.

"It looks just like me," said Joey, his eyes traveling the length of the wall. "They all do. She obviously didn't forget about me. That was something I always wondered about."

When they came to the final portrait, it appeared as if Joey might touch the painting. An older woman who resembled a female version of Joey stood in a field of flowers wearing a long, flowing, white dress. Her black hair woven with silvery strands was spun into a loose bun on her head, and she held a bunch of daisies in her hands.

"That is the artist's self-portrait," said the woman, who had come up behind them. "She painted it a year before she passed. She was a remarkable artist. Her loss was a great one for the artistic community. Many have tried to buy these paintings, but she was clear that they are to remain here on display. She left a fund to ensure that."

When they walked into the hotel room later after dining alfresco following the gallery, Iris noticed that the adrenaline powering her for the last few days had ebbed. "I'm exhausted," she said. "You?"

"That always happens to me after a case," said Joey. "Sometimes I sleep for days."

"I don't want to cut into our adventure, but a few hours would help." Iris pulled off her clothes and slid into bed. Joey did the same, pulling her close and kissing the top of her head as they both drifted off to sleep.

. . .

The clock on the bureau read 3 a.m. Iris looked back up at the ceiling, wondering how this was going to work with Joey. Especially for Jake. She tried to picture what her son's first meeting with Joey might look like, when his voice broke into her reverie.

"We can take this really slow." Iris turned and met Joey's eyes in the dim light. "If you don't want to tell your mom and Jake right away, I understand. I won't press you."

Iris marveled at how he could read her mind just like that. "Thank you. I do want to take it slow introducing you to Jake, and my mom."

"I'll wait as long as it takes. Whatever's best for you. For us."

"Do you see that? Us together?" asked Iris.

Joey was quiet for a moment. "Do you?"

"You first," said Iris.

"I hope so."

Iris put a hand on Joey's chest. "Make love to me."

The moonlight was enough for Joey to take in the sweetness of Iris's face, her seductive body, the look in her eyes that days ago he had only hoped for. A bloom of light caressed her cheek and Joey pulled her to him. "I love you," he said, unable to quiet the words as his heart stuttered in his chest. He longed to make love to her, but he wanted every part of Iris. So they lay like that for the longest time, him stroking her beautiful hair, kissing her from time to time to remind himself he wasn't dreaming. Iris wound her legs in his, and he felt his toes with hers. He wanted to laugh with the joy he felt, but afraid she would confuse its meaning, instead mouthed her name over and over because he loved the sound of it. She kissed her own name on his lips and as she lay her head on his chest, drew a heart in its center. In the middle of the heart she drew an I, then a J, smoothed her fingers over them to send shivers through Joey's body.

"You'll always be mine," he said, and felt her nod her head. "Forever?"

"Yes." She pressed her body tight against his, whispering the word so softly he barely heard it.

Then he explored every part of her with his mouth, his hands, her body growing hot and moist, wet glistening on her skin.

As natural as if they had been loving one another forever, he rose up and moved on top of her. He caressed her breasts, tasted her neck, kissed her mouth long and hard, slid his hand to explore her most intimate part. She loved and stroked him between her palms making him moan, then lifted her buttocks and helped him in the dark. He clasped her by the hips as he drove himself into her, again and again. When he could wait no longer and as his muscles quivered, he gave Iris the whole of him.

Afterward, as he fell on the bed beside her, she stretched the length of her body on his like a cat. Then Iris said the sweetest words he was sure he'd ever heard. "I love you, too, Joey."

EPILOGUE

Joey and Iris's story is complete, but Sammy's is just beginning...

Sammy glanced around the coffee shop. The woman said to meet her here at 9 am sharp. Just then, a woman walked out of the bathroom. She wore a red gauze skirt and white blouse. A long side ponytail reached to her waist. When the woman glanced up and met Sammy's eyes, she gestured to a table against the back wall.

"Good, you came alone," said the woman, her green eyes making a quick assessment of Sammy. "Sit down."

Sammy seated herself across from the woman. "Where did you say you heard about me? And what's your name?"

"A mutual friend," the woman said, pushing a laptop across the table to Sammy.

"This is the computer with the encrypted files?"

The woman nodded. "Unencrypt them, and there will be a handsome payout."

The woman's accent sounded foreign. "Where are you from?" Sammy asked as she opened the computer.

"Nowhere in particular. How long will this take?"

"Not long. What's the password?"

The woman plunked a dark red canvas bag on the table, rummaging around until she pulled out a napkin with words scribbled in black ink. She handed it to Sammy. It smelled of clove cigarettes.

Sammy entered the password, and the home screen came up. She checked the file directory. "Any idea what kind of files I'm looking for? Financials? I see a few different encrypted files here."

"Look for something about Lithuania."

"You're Lithuanian?"

"You talk a lot for a hacker." The woman's eyes flashed in irritation.

"Sorry, I'm not much of an early bird. It'd be nice if I could get a cup of coffee."

The woman stood and headed for the barista before Sammy could tell her what she wanted. Fine, she thought. Just get this job done and get the money so she and Twitch could pay the rent. She located the files the woman wanted and took out her flash drive to transfer them to her computer for unencrypting.

A coffee appeared next to Sammy then, and the woman hissed, "What are you doing?"

"I have to transfer the files onto my computer so I can unencrypt them. Don't worry, I'll erase them as soon as I'm done."

The woman sat down across from her. "Go ahead. Don't take all day about it."

Sammy began unencrypting the files, taking a sip of coffee as she did so. Black. No sugar or cream. Yuck.

"Thanks for the coffee," she said.

Once she finished transferring the files back onto the woman's computer, Sammy turned the laptop toward her. The woman's eyes widened in interest, and she smiled. Closing the laptop, she put it in her bag.

"I trust you erased the files from your computer."

"Sure did," said Sammy.

The woman appeared to hesitate and opened her mouth to say something when the bell on the front door jingled. She glanced over Sammy's shoulder and her eyes widened. Setting an envelope down on the table, she grabbed her bag and hurried out the back door.

Sammy reached over and picked up the envelope, which seemed thin. She pulled out a slip of paper that read, *consider the coffee as payment.* That bitch. Good thing Sammy hadn't erased those files.

See what happens with Sammy in *Discovered Distractions*...

A NOTE FOR YOU

Dear Reading Gem,

Thanks for spending time with me, Joey and Iris! While each of the books in the Discovered Truth Series can be read as a standalone, it's fun to experience the progression and get to know the characters. The series progresses as minor characters introduced in each book become main characters in subsequent books. It's exciting to see what they'll do next!

The Discovered Truth series features complex, gutsy women and equally complicated, charismatic men who find themselves immersed in dangerous and intriguing modern-day challenges, such as human trafficking, drug smuggling, national security threats, and identity theft. When the heroine and hero meet, worlds collide and sparks fly, kindling unforgettable romance and intrigue.

If you like the series, please leave a review on any book review platform. Your opinion matters and is incredibly powerful.

Thanks again and talk soon!

STAY ENLIGHTENED

Thanks for reading! Let's stay in touch. In appreciation of you, I post updates, insider information, and sneak peeks of upcoming books on my website at https://www.juliebawdendavis.com/fiction. You can also email me at Julie@JulieBawdenDavis.com, follow me on Facebook, and find me on Amazon.

Even better, you can join my VIP Reading Gems mailing list here. I also created a Facebook group especially for you! Join Julie's Reading Gems to get the inside scoop on what's going on with the Discovered Truth Series. Find out how characters are created, and what they might do next. I also ask for Reading Gem opinions on upcoming covers and even plot twists. And there are contests and giveaways!

Escape to Unforgettable Romance and Intrigue...

BOOKS IN THE DISCOVERED TRUTH SERIES

Discovered Beginnings:
(FREE at https://www.juliebawdendavis.com/fiction)
Discovered Secrets
Discovered Memories
Discovered Indiscretions
Discovered Liaisons
Discovered Betrayal
Discovered Denial
Discovered Distractions
Discovered Deception
Discovered Lies
Discovered Vengeance
Discovered Redemption
Discovered Obsession
Discovered Transgressions
Discovered Suspicion
Discovered Escape
Discovered Promises
Discovered Cover-up
Discovered Intentions

Box Sets

The Discovered Truth Series Box Set Books 1-4
The Discovered Truth Series Box Set Books 5-8
The Discovered Truth Series Box Set Books 9-12
The Discovered Truth Series Box Set Books 13-16